SUMMER OF MEMORIES

Also by this author:
  Summer of Friends

Visit us at *www.rhpa.org* for more information on Review
and Herald products.

SUMMER OF MEMORIES

▲▲▲▲▲▲▲▲▲ **Tanita S. Davis** ▲▲▲▲▲▲▲▲▲

ℛ

REVIEW AND HERALD® PUBLISHING ASSOCIATION
HAGERSTOWN, MD 21740

The author assumes full responsibility for the accuracy of all facts
and quotations as cited in this book.

This book was
Edited by Raymond H. Woolsey
Cover designed by PierceCreative/Matthew Pierce
Cover illustration by Norman Adams
Electronic makeup by Shirley M. Bolivar
Typeset: 11/13 Veljovic

PRINTED IN U.S.A.

04 03 02 01 00   5 4 3 2 1

R&H Cataloging Service
Davis, Tanita S.
    Summer of memories.

    I. Title.

              813.54

ISBN 0-8280-1393-4

Contents

CHAPTER 1

Calling All Camp Staff . . .

Dear Dannielle:

I hope you've had a wonderful school year and are still planning to join the staff at Lupine Meadows this summer. The position of assistant program director remains open, if you're still interested. Eva Davies has agreed to continue as our program director.

We enjoyed having you last summer, and I know that you will continue to be a blessing to both staff and campers. Please read the attached contract, sign and return it, and we hope to see you at Lupine Meadows at 0600 hours, June 15.

Your friend,

Robert Ahrens

Director, Lupine Meadows Camp

Danni hugged her arms to her body and shivered. The skin on her legs was puckered into tiny goose bumps. Her teeth were chattering. Even her hair was cold.

"Is this what the weather is going to be like all summer?" she asked no one in particular. Kevin, from beneath the hood of his car, just grunted. Roseanne glanced back at her from where she was holding a flashlight for Kevin.

"I really hope not. You look like you're frozen. Why don't you put on a coat or something?" Roseanne looked critically at Danni's hunched body.

"Because I'll be done in just a minute and we can get back in the car." Kevin sounded a little irritated. Roseanne turned on him.

"Kev, you've said that three times. Why don't you just admit that you don't know what's wrong so we can find a phone somewhere?"

Now Kevin was irritated. "Rosey, *I told you,* there are no phones out here!" His face was flushed with frustration. "Danni, please try to start it again."

Danni lurched over to the car, her muscles unwilling to cooperate. She slid into the interior of the vehicle. "Ready?"

"Wait guys, wait." Roseanne came around to the window. Kevin straightened and scratched his nose, giving his face another smudge of grime. He walked over to the window on the other side.

"Let's pray," Rosey suggested.

"I've been praying," Kevin sighed.

"Well, let's pray together," Roseanne persisted. "I feel like it would help."

Danni smiled weakly. She had been praying since the car had overheated and had hissed and clanked to a stop at the side of the road. She had been praying since they had left her home. She wasn't sure what one more prayer would do.

"Help me have faith," Danni prayed silently. Out loud she said, "Well, let's do it."

Roseanne reached for her left hand, while Kevin

reached in through the window for her right. Danni grinned. The Birton twins were still on the same wavelength, even when they were angry with each other. Kevin cleared his throat and she hastily bowed her head.

"Lord, it's me," Kevin began. "I thank You for letting us get this far on our journey. If it's Your will, we pray that we can continue now. Please make my car start, Lord. Thanks. Amen."

Danni fought back a smile at Kevin's brevity. Although he spoke to her more than he had before last summer, he was still a guy of very few words, compared to Roseanne's chattiness. Danni decided that God knew what Kevin meant, even if he didn't say everything out loud.

Roseanne prayed, "Thank You, God, for hearing us. Thank You for giving us the chance to work another summer at Lupine Meadows. Please keep us safe on the remainder of our journey, we ask in Jesus' name, Amen."

Danni frowned slightly. Why hadn't Rosey prayed for the car to start? Did she think that it was already fixed? She found herself envying Roseanne's belief. Suddenly she had to find out.

"I'm starting it," she announced quietly. Kevin wearily raised his head. Danni turned the key in the ignition and gently pressed the gas pedal. There was a *click,* then silence. Danni tried again.

"Give it more gas," Kevin instructed her. He retreated back under the hood. Rosey gave her shoulder a reassuring squeeze before joining him at the front of the car.

Danni tried to find her faith as she tried one more time to start the car.

"Please, if it's Your will," she whispered. She turned the key and gave a vigorous stomp on the gas pedal. At first there was no sound. Then the engine turned over.

Kevin whooped. "We got it! Yes! Yes!" He did a wild little dance. Danni pressed on the gas pedal again, and

9

the engine revved. Roseanne scrambled into the passenger seat. "Come on, Kev!" she yelled.

Danni slid out of the car and into the back seat as Kevin took the driver's seat.

"Thanks, God," he exclaimed when he got in. Danni added her silent thanks.

"And thank you, Danni," Kevin caught her eyes in the rearview mirror as he pulled back onto the road. Danni grinned and felt silly at his smile.

"And, last but not least, thank you, Bessie," he gave his steering wheel a pat.

"Bessie?" Danni laughed. "You named your *car?*"

Rosey snorted. "This car is his baby. You should have seen what it looked like at the beginning of the school year. Kevin's been slaving over this thing forever. I'm surprised he doesn't cover it with a blanket at night."

"I do," Kevin said loftily. "I have to cover it at camp, anyway. I don't want some tree to get sap on it and ruin the paint job."

"Oh, please," Rosey shot back. "Your 'paint job' is a joke. This car is mostly rust!"

"But it is a classic pile of rust," Danni interjected with mock seriousness. "Let's not forget that."

Kevin rolled his eyes and good-naturedly ignored them both.

The past winter had been good to the trio of friends. Kevin had finished his junior year in high school on the honor roll. His tall frame had stretched out even taller, and he was rapidly heading for the 6' 4" mark. The baseball cap that had been his trademark the summer before had been replaced by a black leather Stetson hat. "It goes with your new image," Roseanne had teased.

Roseanne had grown a new confidence over the school year through her participation in the debate team and in student government. She had served as the religious vice president for the student association at the small Christian school where she and her brother attended, and had found her relationship with God growing stronger every day. She seemed ready to take on the challenges of working closely with the campers she loved.

Danni had seen the changes in Roseanne and Kevin while spending time with them in the youth group at church. She and Kevin had kept in touch throughout the school year and had spent time nurturing the spark of special friendship that had sprung up between them the summer before. Danni hoped that there would be time over the summer for the three of them to become even closer, for she had found Rosey to be a wisecracking, fun companion as well.

The miles flew by, and Danni started to think about what lay ahead. She had truly missed Eva and Gloria those first few weeks after camp! Lena and Darla had spent time with her and Roseanne before heading off to their hometowns and schools. Darla had actually gone to a boarding school, and had written infrequent but friendly letters to Danni about how she was doing there. Bill and Glenda had kept in touch; Glenda still thought Bill was one of the most special people that she knew, while Bill still was oblivious to her interest. Perry sent a cryptic note when he had been home sick with bronchitis, and said he was tired of winter and couldn't wait to see her again. David sent her a funny Christmas card and called her to tell her that he had been accepted into medical school.

Danni smiled to herself. Another summer with friends. She couldn't wait to get there.

Kevin flicked another glance into the rearview mirror in time to catch Danni's smile.

"What're you laughing at?" he teased. "Looking forward to cleaning more bathrooms?"

Danni made a face. "Yuck. Every time I cleaned our bathroom this winter I thought of those bathrooms. I really hope that somebody else gets the job this summer!"

"Not a chance," Roseanne grinned. "You guys did *such* a good job."

Kevin and Danni groaned in unison, then laughed.

Yes, another summer with friends. As they wound through the woods on the narrow road, Danni could hardly wait.

CHAPTER 2

Fortune Cookies

Friends were reunited in the cafeteria at supper. Danni, with one arm linked through Darla's, searched for other familiar faces. Her eyes alighted on a short girl with long, wavy black hair and a hesitant look on her face. Danni watched her for a moment, then turned and poked Lena, who was leading the way to a table.

"Who's that?" Danni motioned with her chin.

Lena glanced at the girl and shrugged. "New staff," she replied, scanning the crowd. "Has anyone seen Perry yet, or Tina?"

"Nope," Roseanne answered, then waved happily to someone across the room.

Danni watched the tumult with a warm feeling in her heart, but could not help noticing that there were several people who appeared not to know anyone. She remembered last summer when she had been a newcomer, and Eva had piloted her through the introductions and made things easier. She turned decisively to Darla and Lena.

"OK, guys," she began, "this is how we're going to start this summer. Let's meet the new people. Anyone want to be in my greeting committee?"

Lena laughed. "Are you scoping out the new guys already? What happened to Kevin?"

Danni swatted at her. "Be nice, or I won't help you find Perry," she sassed back.

Darla made a slow turn and surveyed the crowded room. "I spot at least five people who look lost," she reported.

"Good," Danni nodded, satisfied. "Let's start with her." She led the way to the dark-haired girl.

"Hi," said Danni, sticking out a hand. "I'm Dannielle Mallory. This is my second summer here. Where are you from?"

"Hi," the girl replied hesitantly, coloring slightly. "My name is . . . ," she stalled, "is Lee Winn."

"Nice to meet you," Danni replied, automatically, frowning slightly. As more introductions were made, she studied the other girl. Her face was round and her eyes were almond shaped. A smattering of freckles gave her a mischievous look. Danni ventured a question.

"Where are you from, Lee?"

"Uh . . . up near . . . um, by Lakeview," the girl stuttered, blushing slightly.

Danni decided that she had better not try pushing the girl further. "Well, again, it's nice to meet you," she nodded brightly. "Hope to see you around."

Lori Ann, a lifeguard Danni had met the previous summer, stopped and gave her a squeeze.

"You look great!" Danni told her, admiring her short pixie haircut.

"Thanks," returned Lori Ann. "It'll be a lot easier to keep up with this summer."

Darla led the way to the next newcomer, a tall Filipino boy with a swatch of dark hair hanging in front of his eyes.

"Well, hey." He grinned at them with no trace of shyness. "You the welcoming committee?"

Lena's wit rose to the surface. "Are you in need of a welcome?" she teased.

"I sure am," he replied. "I'm Victor Gerardo. Who are all of you?"

"Well, I'm Lena, this is Roseanne . . ."

"I'm Darla," Darla cut in on Lena's recitation, "and this is Danni, and we'd better sit down 'cause here comes Mr. Ahrens!"

"Come sit with us," Lena urged Victor.

Danni caught sight of Eva and Lee Macomber at the next table and gave them each a quick hug before she sat down.

"Welcome, everyone, welcome!" Mr. Ahrens' booming voice filled the room.

"I hope that all of you are settled in and comfortable in your quarters. We have a lot to do throughout this week, and we really need to get started. Let's take a moment to ask the Lord's blessing on our food before we get started. Bill, would you honor us?"

Danni felt a pang as she watched Bill Wright stand and bow his head. It was at her first meal at camp the previous summer that she had met one of her best friends, David Taylor. David was busy taking summer school classes and would be able to join the group only for the last two weeks of the summer.

"Who'd they get to do arts and crafts this summer?" Darla wanted to know immediately after the blessing was said.

"Her—right over there." Lena pointed in the direction of a tall, grey-haired woman sitting at the Ahrens table. "Her name is Beverly Johnson, and she's a member of our church in Minden."

"It's nice to see a lot of new faces here, but I'm really going to miss David this summer," Roseanne sighed.

"So will Eva," Danni laughed. "I have a feeling that he'll pop up every so often this summer during the weekends."

"Where is Perry?" Lena fretted to herself. "I cannot believe that he is late the very first day back!"

"I hope nothing's happened to him," Danni blurted, then wished she hadn't.

"Well, let's not worry," Roseanne said smoothly, turning to Victor. "So, where will you be working this summer?"

"Probably everywhere. I'm going to be doing sub-counseling and some lifeguarding at the pool. And you?" His dark eyes held a curious expression.

"Just about the same. I'll mostly be subbing out at the new Waves program, since I can drive a boat. I cannot wait to get out there on the water."

"Sounds fun," Victor commented.

"Maybe you'll get some time out there as well, if you have your lifeguarding certificate," Lena encouraged him.

Standing in line, Danni studied the faces around her. She saw Suzanne, looking delicate with her peaches-and-cream complexion and dark hair, and ventured a friendly wave. Her movement attracted the girl's companion, who turned and saw her. Jewel-green eyes registered Danni's presence coolly. Danni lifted her hand reluctantly.

"How was your school year, Kat?" she said to the auburn-haired girl.

"Well, it's *you* again!" Kat drawled exaggeratedly, lifting a thin shoulder. She tossed her coppery mane and shrugged. "My year was the usual—," she used an expletive.

Danni jerked inwardly and nodded stupidly, flushing. Kat was up to her usual attitude already.

"Kat, you'd better watch your mouth," she forced the words.

Kat gave her an incredulous look through narrowed eyes. "Grow up," she snorted, and turned away.

Danni rolled her eyes and grimaced. "I have not missed that," she muttered to herself.

Egg rolls and rice with delicious glazed vegetables were on the menu for the evening.

"Man, you could get spoiled here," Victor smacked his lips appreciatively.

"Or fat," Darla moaned disconsolately, holding her full belly.

"As if!" Danni mimicked Kat's voice and laughed.

"Now comes the part I've been waiting for," Lena confided to the group. "You were a 'kitchen kid' last summer. Any ideas on what we get for dessert, Roseanne?"

She shrugged wordlessly, eyes on the kitchen doors, as a slight commotion turned their attention to the front.

"Fortune cookies!" Darla chortled at she watched Mr. Ahrens and the kitchen staff glide in with laden trays.

"Fortune cookies?" Danni frowned slightly. "Are you kidding? Those things are a waste of the energy it takes to eat them!"

"Oh, hush." Lena waved an impatient hand at her as she reached out for her cookie.

"Only one?" Victor looked disappointed. The kitchen helper smiled mysteriously and moved away quickly.

"What's your fortune?" Roseanne peered over Danni's shoulder.

"This is the goofiest thing—mine says 'Violets are blue,'" Lena blurted from the other side of the table.

"Mine says 'Pansies are sometimes purple,'" Darla laughed.

"So does mine!" Victor grinned.

"'Roses are red' over here," Danni waved the tiny scrap of paper. "This must be a game of some kind."

"Aren't you supposed to know, Miss Assistant Program Director?" Roseanne teased her as she eagerly opened her cookie.

17

Danni stuck out her tongue. "Just tell us what you are, smart alec," she replied. Roseanne's face clouded as she looked at her "fortune."

"Green!" she complained in an offended voice. "Shouldn't I have red or something? Danni, would you trade with me, please?"

"Yeah, yeah, now I'm good for something," Danni complained good-naturedly. "Here, take the red one. For all you know, you're jumping from the frying pan into the fire."

"What's this about, anyway?" Victor craned his neck around to see the response of those at other tables to the mysterious "fortunes" they had just received.

"There's Perry!" Lena squealed, abruptly unfolding her lanky frame. "Let's go see him!"

"Wait," Roseanne counseled. "Ahrens is about to make an announcement."

Darla cast a quick look over at the front of the room where Ahrens stood. She waved a frantic hand toward Perry before settling in with a look of mock attention.

Mr. Ahrens laughed as he caught the movement. "We'll wait, Mr. Bowman, for you to find a seat before we begin," he said.

Danni noted that he didn't seem upset that Perry was so late.

Perry threaded his way through the tables. He was greeted enthusiastically with hugs and slaps on the back as he made his way to their group.

"What took you so long?" hissed Lena as Perry finally sat down.

"I got here as soon as I could." He gave her a fierce hug, then coughed. "Details later."

"Now that the last sheep is in the fold," began the camp director, "we should take an opportunity to look around. There are many new faces." There were nods as he continued. "In an effort to get to know each other better this summer, and to further ignite the spirit of Christ's love in all our hearts, we have come up with a concept that we call PowerPacks. A PowerPack is a prayer group, but we hope that they will come to mean so much more to you . . ." He smiled at them for a moment.

"The Bible says in the book of Acts, chapter one and verse eight, that we will receive power when the Holy Spirit comes upon us, and that we will be the Lord's witnesses to the ends of the earth. Jesus Christ is our source of power in this world, and during your time at Lupine Meadows this summer I want you to know Him better. I want you to serve Him better, as you've never served Him before. I want the light of the Lord Jesus that shines through you to touch our campers, and to set their hearts on fire for Jesus. I don't want you just to do the right things and say the right things, but I want you to be impressed in your hearts to do the right things for the right reasons. I don't know about you, but I want to be a witness for the Lord."

"Amen," agreed Victor and several others, startling Danni. Victor grinned at her as she shot him a glance.

"Well, don't let me start preaching," Mr. Ahrens chuckled. "Let's get started. Eva?"

Danni smiled as Eva stepped to the microphone. There was a good-natured laugh as she took a moment to adjust it to her short stature. Danni was always amazed to see how really short Eva was. Her personality carried with it a presence that more than made up for her 5'2" height.

"All right, has everybody had a chance to look over their little cookies? Good. Let's split up, then. 'Violets are blue' to my right here, with our staff nurse, Gloria Rodriguez."

Gloria stood up, clutching a plastic purple flower between her teeth. She made a deep bow as the members of her group joined her.

"Gotta go," said Perry, coughing slightly.

"Oh, great, you're in my group!" Lena bubbled. She linked her arm through his as they started off.

" 'Roses are red' to my left with Bev Johnson, our arts and crafts director." Eva waved in the direction of the tall woman with the generous smile.

"Those of you who are pansies—and don't take that personally—" Eva stopped to chuckle at the pun—"find Darren Irwin, our boys' director, in the back left corner of the room." Darren waved a casual arm. Victor stood and nodded to him as a grin spread itself out over his face. He made his way across the room and the two of them stood chatting like old friends. Darla trailed behind him.

"Finally, emeralds, you'll find Mrs. Ahrens at the back of the room. If everyone would find a seat, dessert is about to be served."

Glenda bounded forward as Danni approached Mrs. Ahrens' table.

"Hey, bud!" Danni gave her a tight squeeze. "I'm glad we get to be together. Isn't it a bummer, though, that the kitchen kids never get to do stuff like this?"

"They have their own PowerPacks—they just meet at different times than we do. Don't worry—they'll have just as much fun as we will."

"Oh, good," Danni responded warmly. She looked around the group. Shy Lee Winn was hanging out on the fringes of the crowd. Danni beckoned to her.

"Hey, Lee! Come sit here," she called. Lee looked at her gratefully and made her way over.

"This is Lee Winn," Danni said, making introductions. Glenda greeted the new girl pleasantly, and engaged her in talk about her home town. Danni studied the girl's delicate features. Despite the freckles and her mane of curly brown hair, Danni decided her new acquaintance was of Asian descent. Her eyes had an exotic look to them.

Mrs. Ahrens interrupted the group with a quiet clearing of her throat. She smiled at the assembled team, her blue eyes glowing with a quiet excitement. Danni thought that she looked like she had a secret.

"Well, everybody, this is it," she said with a smile. "My name is Marguerite Ahrens; you can call me Marty or Marge. I am looking forward to meeting with all of you this summer in our PowerPack." She gazed around the group.

"Let's introduce ourselves. Lyly, I'll start with you."

Leelee? Danni turned curious eyes toward the girl next to her.

"I'm going by Lee." Embarrassment flamed in her face.

"I beg your pardon, Lee," Marge said courteously in her alto voice. An awkward silence followed. Lee looked blankly at the table top.

"Who's next?" Marge asked the question briskly. Danni volunteered information about herself. Her comments were followed by Glenda; then a tall, tanned boy in hiking boots named Tim; a tall African-American girl named Shyanne; Esther Marshall and Mike Hoyt from last summer; and several others. At the close of their hasty introductions, dessert arrived.

As they enjoyed their ice cream and fruit sauce, Mrs. Ahrens told them more about the PowerPack.

"We'll be meeting every Sunday morning after the busses pull out, a little before staff meeting," she told them. "These meetings will be to talk about our week, to mention problems or needs that we have, and to bring our concerns before the Lord in prayer. The bonus for you all"—her eyes twinkled—"is that not only do you get a chance to chat and to get to know each other better, but also I have been begged to bring some of my famous cinnamon buns, so you'll get an extra dose of sugar before the week begins."

Glenda, a true connoisseur of Marge's baking, applauded.

After a cheerful campfire and more introductions of new staff members, Danni climbed the hill to her quarters. This summer she had a room with the other lead staff because of her official status as assistant programming director. Her roommate, named Winona, was someone who hadn't yet arrived when she had gone to dinner. Now Danni opened the door to her room cautiously. The lights were dimmed and it appeared that no one was inside.

"Hello?" she called quietly, suddenly missing the bustle and chatter of the general staff quarters.

No reply answered her hesitant greeting. She shrugged and dressed for bed, taking a few moments to brush out her wavy, light-brown hair. She was lonely, and missed her family—even her goofy older brother, Bart. She dug through her half-unpacked book bag and extracted her Bible. Opening the cover, she pulled out the family photo her father had tucked in before Kevin and Roseanne had picked her up. Looking at Bart's friendly grin, Betti's sweet expression, and her father's craggy, loving features, Danni felt an intense desire to be with them—where she belonged. Looking at the empty bed across from her, Danni felt a yawning chasm of emptiness opening before her. She nervously smoothed out her bed sheets, then determinedly opened her Bible once again. Despite feeling out of sorts, she was anxious not to break her newly started practice of reading for a few moments from God's Word each night before she slept.

Randomly she opened to the Gospel of Matthew and paged along until she came to chapter 25. She sank into the familiar litany of the words: "And at that time, the kingdom of heaven will be like ten virgins who took their lamps . . ."

She looked up several moments later as a light breeze lifted her hair. An outdoorsy smell of dew and pine trees filled the air as her roommate swirled into the room. Danni was at a loss to describe her. She got the impression of a wild animal—round, liquid eyes; long, straight limbs, wildly curly brown hair. She half rose from the bed to introduce herself.

"Don't let me interrupt," Winona said before Danni could get a word out. "I know how it is to be in the middle of a good passage and have to stop. We have all summer to chat." She hauled her suitcase onto her bed and started to unpack into the chest of drawers on her side of the room.

Danni sat back down and by sheer force of will finished the chapter. The scripture had left her with plenty to think about, but she turned her attention to her new roommate for a moment more. She watched as the girl unpacked a huge camera, rolls of film, and several different lenses.

"I guess you're the photographer this summer," she made an easy guess. Winona responded with a half smile. She continued to find a place for her things. Danni tried again.

"Is this your first summer at Lupine Meadows?"

Winona shook her head. Finally her whirl of activity stopped as she sat on the bed and put her attention on

Danni. "I've actually worked here on and off for two summers before this one. I'm sort of an itinerant photographer—I like to hike around and camp and wander the countryside looking for really good nature shots. During the year I work for a photography studio and live with my mom. That's the story." She took a deep breath and looked frankly at Danni.

A little startled at Winona's rapid-fire style of conversation, Danni made an effort to be polite.

"I guess you know my name, Dannielle Mallory," she began, "and I work in programming with Eva. This is my second summer. Um . . ." Danni realized that she had run out of steam already. Fortunately, her roommate saved her by asking her questions. Danni recovered enough to ask Winona, or Nona, as most people called her, some questions of her own. By the time they got the lights out Danni had learned that Nona had some Native American heritage in her family and that her next-favorite love, after photography, was Native American lore. And Danni also discovered that Nona was dating the Native Village director, Jay Dunstan.

"That's where I was tonight—taking pictures of the village in the dark. There's only the Buffalo Tepee up for now, and it looks so neat with just a white moon above it, and a black sky . . ." her voice grew muffled as she turned her head on her pillow. "I should really have worked at the Native Village this summer." She sighed and wished Danni a good night.

Danni lay awake for a while, bemused. Already the summer was full of different characters. She realized that she would have a wonderful summer—sure, a different kind of summer than she had had the previous year, but a wonderful summer nonetheless. People could seem as individual as their faces but underneath there was a common thread that united them all—their very God-given humanness.

And with this reassuring thought in mind, Danni finally went to sleep.

CHAPTER 3

Along the Road

Early morning staff meeting had the look of a Red Cross disaster area. Groggy staff members reclined on counters, chairs, and floor in the staff room. Danni counted at least 20 people wearing hats, herself among them.

"Hail to the unbrushed!" Eva, sporting a cap of her own, tapped Danni's hat brim.

"Morning," Danni broke off with a yawn. "I almost came in my PJ's. I didn't remember 6:45 coming so early last summer."

Eva laughed. "You'll get used to it, my friend. Pretty soon we'll be coming to worship showered and dressed and ready to roll."

"Not likely," muttered Danni.

After worship Danni was approached by a staff member she almost didn't recognize. She, Darla, and Lena were chatting about their hopes for the summer, and Darla was in mid-laugh when she looked over Danni's shoulder and toned down her grin. Surprised, Danni turned around to see a wide-shouldered young man in a buckskin shirt and jeans behind her. She hesitated for a moment as her mind scrolled through possible names, and then she remembered.

"Jay, how are you?" She reached out her hand to shake his. Jay responded by clasping her whole arm in Native American fashion. Deep dimples bracketed his wide grin.

"I hear that you're the Native Village director this summer," Lena greeted him. "How does that feel?"

"Great," Jay grinned again, "except that I don't know what I'm doing. I was just coming to ask you if I could have some help from you and Eva sometime this week in planning for our campfire nights. When the other camps come to visit us I'd like to have a really neat program for them to see."

"I'm sure that will be no problem," Danni assured him, hoping that it wouldn't be. "I'll talk to Eva about it today."

Jay nodded in an almost courtly fashion, then walked away on moccasined feet. With another strange feeling, Danni watched him go.

"Boy," Darla blurted, "has he changed over the past year!"

"Really," agreed Lena. "This year he seems to have more . . . presence."

Danni nodded silently; in her mind Jay seemed to stand taller and walk with more authority since becoming the Native Village director. It was almost as if the guy who last summer was always followed by a dusty gaggle of little kids with feathers in their hair no longer existed. In his place there was a regal chieftain.

"He's really taking his job seriously," Danni finally said. "Like my roommate."

"Your roommate?" the conversation picked up again. "What's she like?"

The girls walked back to their separate quarters discussing who they had seen and who they missed from the previous summer. Perry called to them from the kitchen patio, and they meandered over to sit with him in the sunshine.

"Taking a break already?" Lena teased. "What's the matter, no Outpost campers to feed yet?"

"Hey now, I own this place, don't forget," Perry tilted back his head and let the sun caress his freckled face. The next moment he sat forward and coughed.

"What is with this cold you have?" Danni frowned at Perry. "You've been sick for ages."

Perry shrugged a little shamefacedly. "I'm allergic to Lena," he mocked, and ducked away from her flailing hand.

Danni could see that this conversation was going to end as most of them did—with Lena doing her best to beat Perry up, and him crying for mercy and protection from anyone who walked by. She giggled. Some things never did change, and the love/hate relationship between Perry and Lena was one of those things. She wondered why they never seemed to become more than friends, and she stored that little matchmaking thought away to discuss with herself at a later time.

Her attention was regained by Perry coughing again, gaspingly, as if something was coming up. She frowned and, remembering her first-aid training, just watched until he could safely draw a breath. Then she placed her hands on either side of his neck.

"Perry," she scolded, "we're going to see Gloria right now. You're still sick! Your lymph nodes are even a little swollen." She pulled him into a standing position.

"Those are jaw muscles," he said with offended dignity as he waved them all away and stood up on his own. "And I don't have time to see Gloria right now—I have way too much work to do for breakfast." He waved a dismissing hand at Danni. "Gloria knows when I need something I'll come down to the infirmary. Don't worry about me."

"Well, at least get a drink of water," nagged Danni.

"IwillIwillIwill!" Perry scooted away from them, back to the kitchen.

Eva joined Danni after breakfast to listen to the jobs being assigned. Danni felt odd to realize that she already knew what she would be doing. She and Eva waited to hear who would be assigned to be their assistant for the morning.

"I hope we get to work with Lee this morning," she said while looking around the buzzing room.

"Lee Macomber?" Eva glanced up at Danni.

"No—Lee Winn. Marge called her Leelee or something."

"Oh." Danni had Eva's full attention now. "You mean Lyly Nguyen. She's a nice girl, isn't she?"

"She's kinda quiet," Danni commented. "Why do you guys call her Leelee?"

"That's her full first name—her whole name is Lyly—L-y-l-y N-g-u-y-e-n. She uses what she calls her American spelling, L-e-e W-i-n-n. She's half Vietnamese.

"Oh-h," Danni breathed, understanding. "She does look slightly Asian. I wonder why she doesn't want to go by her real name?"

"I think she's afraid that if people find out that she's Vietnamese, they won't like her."

"But that seems weird," Danni objected. "There are other Asian people at camp—look at Diane Tsu. Everybody knows she's Japanese. And Victor's Filipino."

Eva shrugged. "It has less to do with being Asian and more to do with the Vietnam War. There are still a lot of hard feelings about that from the people who fought in it. And don't let Diane and Victor fool you—they have experienced prejudice too."

Danni thought of her own father, who had fought in the Vietnam War, and wondered how he felt about the whole thing.

"It just seems like the Vietnam War was so long ago—it was over before I was born."

Eva shook her head. "So was slavery. That hasn't made much difference, has it?"

They turned their attention back to the work assignments. Shyanne was chosen to go to the Native Village. She gave a squeal and hugged another girl, Summer, who was going with her. Thinking of the Native Village reminded Danni of her conversation with Jay. She recounted the incident to Eva.

"I think we'll have less help to give Jay than he thinks," Eva remarked. "He is taking on his leadership role so well that I really feel he knows exactly what he's doing. He has plans for the Native Village that we haven't even thought of yet."

Danni's attention was turned as Marge called for assistants for the program room. A tall, wiry boy named Kenneth bounded forward in response to his name being called, and Suzanne followed him reluctantly to Eva's side. Danni noticed that Kat was assigned to Winona to unpack the photography studio and lab.

"Good luck, Nona," muttered Danni under her breath.

"That's better," Eva nodded in satisfaction as the doors and windows to the long basement room were thrown open. Sunlight puddled on the newly swept floor, and the shelves full of costumes and props looked neat and tidy. Danni had wondered why Eva had requested two helpers to organize such a tiny room, but now she understood. Despite the fact that at times they had bumped elbows in the narrow passages—mainly when Kenneth tried to climb a ladder above the cupboard where Suzanne was stacking scripts and band music—the job had been done quickly. It was lunchtime, and the small office that Eva and Danni shared could be tackled that afternoon as they began to plan for campfire.

"Let's see if we can catch up with Gloria," suggested Danni as Eva closed the door to the office.

"Great," she responded, and they started around the building to the infirmary. They found Gloria still unpacking syringes and some sort of tubing.

"Yikes, what's all this?" Danni made a horrible face. "These needles look vicious!"

"Well, if you needed something from one of them, they might not look too bad," Gloria responded distractedly. "Don't talk a minute, hm? I'm counting."

Eva and Danni stood quietly as Gloria made some quick calculations in her head. Danni looked around at all of the posters showing germs with surly faces being warded off by soap and water. She had a feeling that more than one kid would go home that summer with a better handwashing habit.

Gloria looked up. "So, it's time to eat, no? *Una momento,* and I will join you." Gloria opened a drawer in her desk, grabbed a brush, and ran it through her luxurious dark hair. She quickly washed and dried her hands and locked up her office.

"So, how's the studying?" Eva fell into step with Gloria.

Gloria made an exasperated sound. "I don't know if any more studying is going to make a difference," she complained. "I think I know everything, but you know how tests go. Taking the practitioner boards is really important to me, but here I have so many things to concentrate on! I'll be glad when it's over."

"It'll be better during Family Camp," Eva soothed. "You'll have a whole week to study in the afternoons and in the evenings while you're on call. The doctor will take the brunt of the drop-ins, unless there's an emergency."

"Unless—*unless?* Family Camp is nothing but emergencies," Gloria complained good-naturedly.

"Next summer Ahrens is talking about making the joy last for two weeks instead of just one," Eva warned her.

"I won't be here—I don't think I can take any more!"

"At least you didn't throw mop water on anyone," Danni offered. "I'm sure that lady will be looking for me again this year."

"We will have to make sure and keep you away from the bathrooms," Eva teased her.

In the kitchen, Perry scooped melon mounds into the hollowed-out rinds of watermelons. He felt the familiar enemy, exhaustion, creep up on him. He finished his fruit salad with an angry set to his mouth. He was really, really, really tired of being sick. He slammed his metal spoon into the stainless steel sink. Carlotta, the head cook, glanced his way.

"You're looking a little tired, sweetie. Why don't you run out for a break?"

Perry gave her an icy glance and muttered something under his breath. "Perry . . ." Carlotta's voice held a gentle scolding. He sighed and pulled the butcher's apron over his head. He wiped his hands on the white cotton material and walked to the tiny laundry room off the kitchen to deposit his apron into the washer. Every dish towel, apron, serving jacket, and hot pad in the camp kitchen was a spotless, blinding white. It saved on separating laundry loads, Carlotta always said, and bleach could be used on all of it. Perry felt like he was in a snowdrift. He hunched into his vile mood and tried to scoot past the short brunette woman. She held out her arm and stopped him.

"You'll get to feeling better after you see the doctor," she reminded him.

"I know," he sighed. "It's just hard . . ." he shrugged.

"Have patience," she smiled, looking at him with her

head tilted and her eyes full of feeling.

Perry smiled back, unable to stay frustrated under the motherly eyes of his boss and friend.

"I'll be OK, Carlotta," he smiled. "I'm going on my break. Thanks." He slipped out the door.

Danni, Eva, and Gloria passed under the redwood porch into the outdoor eating area. Perry was once again at a table. Gloria veered his direction and gave him a hug.

"How're ya feelin' today?" She smoothed her hand across his shoulder.

Perry shrugged and smiled. "I'm going into town tomorrow," he replied.

"How do you rate a day off already?" Danni gave him an offended look. Gloria glanced quickly from one face to another, her smile dimming slightly.

"This is business, my child, family business." Perry gave her his godfather voice. "Want I should take care of any business for you?" He nodded his chin in Danni's direction.

She rolled her eyes at his theatrics. "The only business I think you should take care of is getting some antibiotics for whatever it is you have. Gloria, you should know that this guy is sick. He really ought to see a doctor."

Perry put a hand on her arm. "I will," he said simply. Gloria glanced at Eva and frowned.

Danni felt victorious. "That was easy," she grinned. She wondered why nobody seemed to share her glee. "Aren't I good?" she asked no one in particular. Perry rolled his eyes and ignored her comment.

"Can you come out and eat with me?" He smiled at the three of them. "There's some fruit salad I made myself"—he gloated proudly—"and the rest of the meal is pretty tasty as well."

"Of course." Eva looped an arm around Danni and Gloria. "We'll go dish up right now."

In the end Lena, Darla, and Glenda joined them. Perry entertained them with jokes and funny memories from the previous summer. Danni found that she was doing more laughing than eating, and forced herself to pay more attention to her food. She noticed that neither Gloria nor Perry was eating. Perry claimed that his throat was so sore that he had trouble swallowing. Danni wished that he would go to a doctor today.

"Hey, aren't you guys coming to the meeting?" Roseanne asked as she trotted up the stairs to the staff assembly room.

"Meeting? Is it 1:30 already?" squeaked Darla as she hastily caught up her tray and raced for the kitchen. The others followed quickly, still chuckling from Perry's antics. Perry made his way toward the kitchen. Danni stopped and gave him a quick hug, marveling at how thin he was.

"Thanks for eating with us, Perry. You always make my day." She jogged up the stairs. Perry's chuckle followed her.

A busy afternoon passed quickly. Eva and Danni spent the afternoon going through their files on melodramas and skits, pulling out possible Friday night options for a play.

"Oh, here's a cute one," Danni broke the silence as she held up a script. "This one's 'Caterpillar and Tadpole.' It's about the changes God makes in us."

"That one is cute," Eva agreed, "but for the Friday night play we really want one that uses more actors than just two main characters. Leave that in the stack for church skits."

"How about 'The Road'"?

"Excellent play. Won't fly with the 8- and 9-year-olds, though—nondrivers."

Danni chuckled and put the play on the Teen Camp stack.

"*Ah ha!* I've got it!" Danni jumped as Eva leaped up and waved a script over her head. "Crosses by Design!"

"What, huh?" Danni stared at her friend blankly.

Eva forced herself to take a deep breath. "Crosses by Design," she repeated. "Like designer crosses. This play is actually the story of the good Samaritan, but it talks about how we see our responsibility as Christians—doing the right things for the right reasons. See, there are several crosses—one really tiny one that can be hidden in a coat pocket, a big padded flowery one that looks like those padded photo albums—you know, lacy and stuff. And then there's a big gilded one . . ."

Eva continued with her description while Danni's mind raced ahead to how many props would be needed for this play, and how the lighting would work. She barely nodded her head when Eva's voice stopped. She sat still for a moment longer, then said, "You know, we'll need to back the floodlights up and have the house lights up for people to exit the stage."

"You're right of course," Eva grinned, and Danni grinned back. It felt exciting to be working together again, and to know that their partnership had not changed.

"Now let's work on casting it," Eva chirped, and Danni groaned

June 18

Dear Betti & Dad & Bart,

Hi! I'm having a blast, as you probably already knew. It's a little weird to be living upstairs with Lead Staff, but it is nice because Eva is at the end of the hallway. Gloria

still lives above the infirmary, but she is studying so hard right now that I am afraid to go and visit her. These boards are really important to her. (Bart, I hope that your studies are going well also. I know it is hard to study in the summer—hang in there, Doctor! It'll be worth it!)

My roommate is really . . . unique. She's totally into crawling around in the woods at all hours to get these excellent shots of some wildflower with dew on it. I have to say that her side of the room definitely has more life in it than mine, but I hardly ever seem to be in here!

Our PowerPack group is having Adventures in Prayer. It sounds like a contradiction in terms, almost, but it really isn't. The way Marge talks about it, prayer really is an adventure. We are taking a type of prayer each week and talking about it. We started out with "Prayer is asking." That seems kind of obvious, but most people pray vague prayers because they're afraid to ask for real. Interesting, huh? We have some really good discussions.

I hope to see you during the week of Family Camp. I don't care when you come, really. Just come and see me! You'll love the changes that have been made. A lot of the staff worked really hard to put in new trails, a go-cart track, and at the Native Village they built a really neat sweat lodge. The Cowboy Outfit has built a new corral with seats built into the fence. And the programs—you will never believe how they start the campfire up at the Native Village—with a flaming arrow! Be afraid! Everything looks really neat . . . now we just wait for campers.

Keep me in your prayers!

Love you all!

A light rain fell Friday afternoon. The clouds had been churning and little eddies of dust had been kicking up all morning. For the first time all week Danni found herself with an extended amount of free time on her hands. After lunch, Mr. Ahrens had announced that the staff had earned a little R&R time, and that from the noon meal until 6:30 they were free to roam the camp, run personal errands in town, or sleep. Winona immediately took advantage of the opportunity to disappear into the woods with a camera around her neck and her cloud of brown hair momentarily tamed beneath a white bandanna. Kevin offered to drive Roseanne, Danni, Darla, and Lena into town to shop for a few things. Danni, not eager to experience Kevin's car again so soon, declined and told them to enjoy themselves. Victor took Shyanne and Summer in his shiny red truck to find a bead shop in town where they could buy materials to decorate the knee-length moccasins they planned to make at the Native Village.

The arts and crafts building was open. Danni peeped in to discover Bev Johnson working busily on a large pitcher and bowl set that she was going to send to her mother. Danni looked with interest at the new ceramic molds that Bev had brought, and chose a few projects that she and Betti could work on during Family Camp. Too restless to start on anything now, she waved goodbye to Bev and continued on her way.

Danni prowled around the pond, remembering disABILITIES camp from the previous summer. She sat for awhile sketching the clouds gathering over the shadowy hills. When the first spatter of rain freckled her paper, she gave up and trekked back to the main lodge, determined to catch a nap.

Curiosity led her to peek into the cafeteria on the way to her room. The dining hall was dim and cool. The shining stainless steel kitchen was empty except for food service directors sitting in their offices, probably planning menus. A little disappointed not to find anyone about, Danni went up the stairs.

The staff assembly room was on the second floor of the main lodge. Piano music rolled out of the door of the large room. Cautiously, reluctant to invade anyone's solitude, Danni stuck her head in the door. Bill Wright sat hunched over the gleaming white keys, eyes closed, playing a gorgeous minuet from memory. Danni filed that piece of information away in her mind for later use. Pianists were often in short supply for camp church services.

Finally entering her own hallway on the third floor, Danni got a surprise in the form of Perry, sitting on the floor in front of Darren Irwin's door. His head was back against the wall, and his eyes were closed. Danni paused a moment, then crept past him and opened her own door.

"So, it's like that, is it?" Perry said clearly, not opening his eyes.

Danni jumped guiltily, then laughed. "Well, I didn't know if you were awake, you silly," she replied, dropping her sketch pad and pencils in the hallway and disappearing into her room. She returned moments later with two pillows, one of which she threw at Perry. He accepted it and stretched out full-length on the hall floor. Danni flopped onto hers in her doorway and propped her head up on her hands.

"Were you waiting for someone?" she wanted to know.

"Nah. I was listening to Bill play for awhile, then decided I needed a nap. Darren lets me crash in his room when I'm too tired to make it down to staff quarters."

"In or *near* his room?" Danni teased him.

"I get as close as I can," he chuckled, opening his eyes again to smile at her.

Danni talked to him quietly as she doodled on her pad, and he answered her without opening his eyes. After some time, she realized that his even breathing indicated that he really had fallen asleep in the hallway. She laughed to herself at the ridiculousness of the situation. "This is something only Perry would do," she told herself. "Who else is goofy enough to fall asleep in the hall because they were too tired to get into bed?"

She took advantage of his stillness to do several good sketches of his face. His exhaustion was apparent. His freckles stood out in high contrast to his milk-white face. Dark circles ringed his eyes, and even in sleep his mouth was bracketed by lines of strain. She watched him for awhile, thinking of Kevin. She wondered what she felt about him . . . and about Perry. Kevin was such a great guy—and he seemed interested in a relationship. Perry was always joking, and Danni couldn't really read him. She sighed. Not trusting herself to scrutinize her feelings any further, she went back to her sketch pad.

Finally, feeling sleepy herself, Danni rested her head on her arm and decided to close her eyes—for just a moment. When she opened them again Perry was gone, and a smiley face was drawn on her sketch pad.

CHAPTER 4

Running With the Angels

Danni felt a tightening in her stomach again as she stood anxiously with the rest of the staff in the parking lot to meet the buses for disABILITY week. She glanced around at the other staff members, noting the confidence in Summer's stance and looking at Shyanne biting her lip. At supper on Friday evening, Shyanne's disability had been blindness. As had been Danni's experience the previous summer, she had had to eat spaghetti with patches over her eyes, and she hadn't appreciated it one bit. Lee had seemed to find the exercise enlightening, for she had mentioned to Danni that she was doubly grateful for her own sight.

Danni looked around for her friend. Lee had finally thawed out some and was making friends with the group. Victor had really gone out of his way to draw her out, and now she actually started conversations with people instead of just hanging out on the sidelines. She spotted Lee standing next to Darla, who would be her cocounselor for the week. She wandered over.

"It seems like they are never going to get here," Darla complained. "I've been wanting Deanna to see this place forever, and they're probably sitting somewhere waiting for the bus to cool down from overheating."

Danni marveled at Darla's casual use of the word "see." Darla' s sister Deanna had been born with a visual disability described as tunnel vision. Her range of sight was diminishing each year, and soon she would be totally blind. Darla had explained that to the new counselors, to give them an idea that being legally blind didn't always mean totally unable to see.

"They aren't actually due to arrive here for five more minutes," she teased Darla.

"I don't think she can make it," Lee said in a stage whisper. Darla swatted at them both.

When the busses finally did pull in, the usual pandemonium ensued. Darla flew forward to pluck Deanna out of the crowd, and give her 11-year-old sister a squeeze. Danni laughed at the resemblance between the two girls. Deanna had wavy brown hair that was cut into a simple bob. Her thick glasses gleamed in the sun. Her laugh sounded exactly like Darla's.

As campers exploded from the crowded busses, Danni kept her eyes peeled for a white blond head of hair and a small stubborn frame. Mari Burtz had been an especially difficult camper the summer before, and Danni had felt that she had failed miserably in her attempt to befriend the girl. An accident during the rodeo had reminded Mari too forcefully of her own fall from a horse, and was responsible for her early return home. Danni sincerely hoped that Mari had decided to try camp again, but after a fourth bus pulled in with no sign of her, Danni knew that she was to be disappointed.

Sighing, she turned and made her way back to the program room. Campfire would not get planned by itself.

The evening was a raving success. The band played well, and the staff led the campers in games designed to get them involved. Danni was exhausted by the time the last child had been herded off to bed. She saw Lee Macomber as she shut off the lights to the program room.

"Hey, Lee! How do things look for this week?" Danni called to her.

"Things are looking great!" Lee responded warmly. "I'm just getting ready to do my first walk through in the cabin area. Want to come along?"

"Sure!" Danni agreed. "I want to see if some of the same girls are here from last summer."

The pair walked on the packed dirt road through the cabin area. Yellow pools of light crisscrossed the trail, and the eager babble of young voices gave melody to the night. Lee stepped onto the porch of the first cabin and knocked.

"Ten more minutes girls," she called out as she poked her head in the doorway.

"What? That's it?" someone shrieked, and an acceleration in activity ensued.

Lee chuckled as she closed the door. "It's the same every night," she said.

A rising sun engraved above a rounded hill adorned the door of Cabin 13. The noise from this cabin was especially loud. Tearful, angry voices sounded from inside. Lee frowned and shook her head.

"Oh, no. I was hoping that these girls would all get along," she sighed as she stepped onto the porch. "This cabin has a lot of girls who have been here before. We were hoping that by putting Mari Burtz in with this lot, she'd be encouraged to have a better time."

"Mari is here?" Danni blurted. "I didn't see her get off the bus!"

"Yes. She missed her bus, so her parents drove her up." Lee stopped a moment to listen to the voices inside the cabin. Danni recognized Jenny Quinn's calming voice, coaching her girls into expressing themselves less hysterically, and Mari's monotone making a response. Lee gave a big grin as quiet descended. After a moment, she knocked on the door.

"Hi, Lee," Jenny greeted her. Terri Pierce, who was cocounseling with Jenny, smiled and waved. Lee gave the girls quiet praise for being almost ready for bed and quiet. They exchanged guilty looks while Tanya, whom Danni recognized from Christine Porter's cabin the previous summer, blinked tear-tangled lashes and looked as if she were still simmering. Danni closed her eyes and shook her head. It was amazing to her that Mari could cause so much trouble wherever she went.

Danni's room smelled like mint when she entered. She undressed quietly, grateful for momentary privacy while Winona was in the bathroom. The minty smell was explained moments later when her roommate emerged with a green mask on her face. Danni bit back a smile. Nona's facials got stranger every night. Last night it had been honey and avocado oil. Tonight it was seaweed and spearmint.

"Where have you been wandering?" Winona asked carefully through a stiffened face.

"I went out to do the cabin walk-through with Lee," Danni replied, her voice muffled through her top.

"Aren't these kids just great?" Nona enthused. "I'm really looking forward to working with some of the sighted kids in the photography lab. I have two cabins tomorrow, right after Camp Council."

"*Two* cabins?" Danni winced. "I hope you asked Marge for an assistant."

"I have one—do you know Kat Armstrong, the red-haired girl who—"

"Kat? She's your assistant?" Danni tried to hide her disbelief. "You work well together?"

"Uh-huh. She's such a sweetie, and Jay says that she's really been helping him out." Nona carefully avoided moving her mouth. Her cheeks cracked anyway. She sighed and got up from her bed to wash off the aromatic plaster.

"That's . . . great," Danni sat on her bed with a bewildered expression. Last summer many of the Lead and Executive staff had had problems with Kat's attitude. She tended to volunteer for jobs and then back out, not finish, or fail to show up. Maybe Kat was changing this summer, for the better.

"She does so much for me," Nona continued, patting dry her rosy face. "Today I left a lens up at the Native Village. Kat went all the way back up there and got it for me. She is always rolling film for me, and she cleans up after we develop in the lab. I wouldn't know what to do without her!"

Danni shook her head in astonishment but did not say anything else. She had long ago decided that people should be allowed to form their own opinions of others. Bart had reinforced this by refusing to answer any questions Danni had about people she didn't know but he did. When entering high school, Danni had asked Bart which teachers to avoid. His refusal to respond had rewarded her with several excellent relationships with teachers whom Bart had struggled to work with.

Danni hoped that this would be Nona's experience. Despite the aggravation that Kat had caused her personally, Danni didn't want to talk behind her back, and hoped that she'd be nice enough to Nona to reassure her that she had done the right thing.

At breakfast the following morning Darla and Lee's cabin caught Danni's attention. They were planning their day while consuming huge quantities of breakfast cake and fresh fruit. Lucretia, whom Danni had met the summer before, was pleased, between bites, to introduce her sister, Lawanna.

"You should hear the two of them sing," Darla marveled. "They get us up in the morning singing away. I think they should become professionals."

"Maybe they can sing a song for Camp Council on Friday," Danni responded with a wink at the counselors.

The table erupted into noisy confusion. "Can't we all do it?" the suddenly shy Lucretia pleaded. Lawanna seconded her motion with a timid nod.

"Sure, we'll look forward to it," Danni chuckled.

Later that morning she related the experience to Eva. "It's too bad that we can't have some sort of talent show for the whole group," she remarked. "They all seem so willing."

"Lupine Meadows is the one place that some of these kids get to shine," Eva responded. "We used to have a talent show every summer, but it got to the point that we had to extend it two nights, then three. For some of the younger fry, it was really hard to sit still for that long."

"Why not do it by cabin?" Danni suggested. "Maybe we could stipulate that there be only one or two acts per cabin. That way we could allow everyone to participate who would like to, but it would make the first audition the responsibility of the counselors. Then, when they're sure of what they want to do, they can audition for us. What do you think?" Danni paused and waited for Eva's response.

Eva nodded meditatively, chewing on her lower lip. "We're going to have to switch a few things around for afternoon activities, and cancel the Frontierland campfire, but I don't think that Jerry and Steve will mind another week to work on their storytelling . . ." her voice trailed off and she started walking again.

Danni, by now used to the way that Eva thought, did

not bother to answer her. In a few moments Eva would have the whole thing planned out and they would move on to something else. Sure enough, after a minute of silence, Eva nodded to herself and remarked that they would announce the event at lunch and have auditions that evening and the following morning.

They crossed the lower meadow toward the huge, spreading oak tree at its center. A split-rail hitching post formed a U-shaped boundary beneath The Tree, as it was commonly called. In the cool green dimness beneath, horses stood tethered, twitching irritated flesh against flies and stamping their hooves impatiently. Danni gave the area a healthy respect. She stood well back from the lines of horses, a little shy of their swishing tails. Eva, on the other hand, walked boldly into the middle of the fray, patting horses familiarly on their flanks, and pushing them aside as needed.

Jim materialized from between two speckled horses. He shoved his hat back on his sweaty head and made a great show of welcoming them to the horsemanship area. Kevin appeared from somewhere behind Danni and dusted off a small stool for her.

While Eva talked to Jim about doing mail call at lunch, Kevin talked to Danni. Both Kevin and Jim were in continuous motion, tightening girth straps, checking bridles and saddles. In a moment it was apparent why they had to keep moving. A small group of impatient children headed across the meadow their way.

Kev pulled a badly creased sheet of paper out of his pocket. After consulting it, he refolded it and nodded to Danni.

"Right on time. This is Jenny and Terri's cabin coming. Wanna ride with us? I think we have a couple extra horses."

Danni, who was not afraid of horses in theory, felt her stomach plunge.

"Uh—no thanks. Mari is in this cabin, and she and I don't do too well together, and I uh . . ." She ran out of excuses for a moment.

Kevin grinned at her. "Don't worry about Mari—I'll have her under wraps. She sounds just like my little sister, Kym. Come on, Danni. Please?"

"Well . . . let's saddle the other kids up and see if we have room first," she replied in a small voice.

Kevin looked at her for a long moment. He opened his mouth to say something when a shrill whinny from a horse caught his attention. He glanced away, then looked back.

"There'll be a horse," he said squeezing her shoulder. "Wait here."

It was a shorter time than Danni could have ever believed before the kids were mounted up. Tanya, looking flushed and excited, was riding on a small black horse with a white blaze on his forehead and white socks. Danni had a moment of anxiety when she saw Mari approach the horses; her fall from a horse's back had cost her full use of her legs. She displayed confidence, however, and chose a tall chestnut mare. Jim assisted her as she mounted.

"I really don't need any help," Mari announced as she settled on the horse's back. "I can ride very well, and I can even jump."

"That's great," Jim said, his face splitting into a genuine smile. "Maybe someday you can work at Cowboy Camp and teach a jumping class."

Mari gave him a scornful look. "Not likely," she replied. "I'm going to Europe and win a steeplechase."

Jim shrugged good naturedly. "That'll be great too,"

he responded cheerfully, and moved on.

Eva decided not to ride out with the group but wait by the tree with one small camper who was terrified of falling off. Danni was to ride at the end of the line with Jenny, while Kevin and Terri took the middle. Jim would ride in the lead. Kevin fished a bandanna out of his pocket for Danni to tie over her mouth and nose on the dusty parts of the trail. He gave her a leg up on a swaybacked white horse who immediately danced sideways skittishly. Danni gripped the saddle horn firmly. Sweat beaded on her forehead. She had no intention of falling off—especially not with Kevin watching.

"Let's mooovvve out!" sang out Jim from the front of the line. He walked his horse around the hitching post and down the trail deeper into the meadow. Many of the campers followed suit, for their horses were used to traveling in a string. Tanya, however, pulled on her horse in vain.

"He won't go," she said to Kevin frantically. "He's stuck."

"Slack up on the reins," Kevin instructed her. "You're pulling him back."

"Oh, good grief, Tanya," Mari remarked, shaking her head. "Can't you even ride a horse?"

"Mari," Jenny said in a firm, no-nonsense voice, "please catch up with the group."

Red-faced, Tanya jerked at her horse's reins, then finally let go altogether. Her horse took a step forward, then broke into a bumpy jog to catch up to the line.

"Yikes!" Tanya squealed, and fumbled for her reins.

Danni reveled in the cool beauty of the green field. Butterflies wheeled in fluttery circles around black-eyed Susans. The poppies were a brilliant orange, and the lupine, which the camp was named for, showed a startling periwinkle blue.

48

The relaxing ride was over too soon. The horses started back up the small incline toward the hitching post. Danni was a little disappointed, but realized that the girls needed to get back in time for mail call and lunch. She was not the only one wishing for a longer ride, and she heard Mari's strident voice from up ahead.

"Is that all? Why don't we go on this trail?"

"Some of the nonsighted campers would find that trail very difficult." Kevin's voice was pleasant. "There are a lot of branches to duck and that sort of thing."

"Well, I'm not blind, and I want to go," snapped Mari. "I can ride, you know."

Kevin blew out a deep breath. Mari had been pushing to trot and gallop and jump for the whole ride. Danni could hear the weariness in his voice.

"Mari, I'm really glad that you like to ride, but I don't think that you understand that we have to plan a ride that everyone in your cabin can take. When you get home you can do that type of riding if you want. There are other weeks in the summer where we do have more advanced rides—and a lot of kids go to Cowboy Camp and learn other skills. For this week, well, you'll have to stay with the pack. Jim and I can't keep up with you!" He tried to lighten the moment with a false chuckle.

Mari withdrew into herself. The rest of the ride passed without more comment from her. Back at The Tree, Danni hopped off her horse and gratefully set her feet on solid ground. She clipped her horse to the post and began to lead other riders to a spot at the fence. Terri flashed her a quick smile as they passed each other, each assisting a camper to a safe distance from the horses where they could unbuckle their riding helmets and start up toward the flagpole area. Eva returned her camper and started back up to her office.

There were several nonsighted campers left to dismount when Danni caught a quick movement out of the corner of her eye. Mari was still astride her horse. Kevin glanced up at her at the same time Danni and Jenny did. Jenny started toward her.

"Let me help you—" Jenny's words were cut off. Mari slapped the reins against the mare's neck and the horse responded. Horse and rider shot off in the direction of the east meadow, toward the Lupine House.

"Mari!" shrieked Jenny, then clapped a hand over her mouth. Horses shifted uneasily. Danni ran and caught the bridle of a horse that tried to follow Mari's, and clipped it securely to the post.

Kevin spun on his heel and launched himself onto his horse. Eyes blazing, he whipped off across the meadow after Mari. "Call Gloria," he yelled as he raced away, clapping his Stetson more firmly on his head.

Jim and Jenny secured the horses while Terri herded the campers to safety. On rubbery legs, Danni ran up the hill toward the infirmary. Jim mounted a horse and rode off in the direction that Mari and Kevin had taken.

"Gloria," Danni yelled through the infirmary door. "Come quick! They might need you down at The Tree. Mari took a horse! Hurry! Hurry!"

Gloria rose from behind her desk. "What?" she asked, closing her textbook.

"Emergency at The Tree," was all Danni could get out.

Immediately Gloria grabbed a first-aid kit. She trotted toward the door, firing questions at Danni.

"Did someone fall off?"

"N-no."

"Stepped on or kicked?"

"No."

Gloria stopped and looked at Danni. "What happened, then? Someone stung by bees or get slapped in the eye with a branch?"

Danni finally found her voice. "Mari Burtz took off on a horse across the meadow."

"She what?" Gloria looked angry.

"She wanted a longer ride," Danni explained, feeling sick. "Kevin rode out after her."

"Oh, no," moaned Gloria. She broke into a run toward The Tree.

Danni reeled with the seriousness of the situation. If Mari fell off of her horse and was injured, Kevin and Jim were going to be held responsible. Despite the fact that Kevin was a good rider, he could still fall off too, or his horse could twist an ankle in a hole, or . . . Sudden, frightened tears came to her eyes.

"Jesus, please do what is best for Kevin and Mari," she prayed out loud as she jogged toward the headquarters building and Mr. Ahrens' office. "Please don't let Kevin get hurt, or Mari either."

Lee Macomber, Marge, and Mr. Ahrens stood quietly at the flag line. Danni had shared her story and had accompanied the anxious group to the meadow, where no sign of Mari, Kevin, or Jim was to be seen.

"They went off toward the woods and we lost sight of them," explained Terri. "I don't know if Kevin caught up with her."

Lee sighed deeply, wringing her hands together in anxiety.

"Well," she said, "we have to leave this in God's hands. There's nothing the rest of us can do right now but wait." She shook her head. "Let's hand out the mail and have the blessing. These kids still need to eat, and so do we." She straightened her shoulders and called out, "Campers, atten—*tion!*"

Mail call went quickly. Mr. Ahrens offered the blessing and included in it a fervent prayer for Mari, Kevin, and Jim's safety. Danni discovered that she had no appetite and sat out on the cafeteria porch, watching the unchanging meadow. Lee sat down next to her silently.

"It's on days like this . . ." she began.

Danni sat forward and looked toward the east end of the meadow. A tiny puff of dust rose near the pond. Her eyes strained as she tried to make out what it could be.

"Is that—" Lee sat forward and peered out across the sunny meadow, shading her eyes.

"Please, God, please," whispered Danni, standing up and squinting. She made out a figure running, leading a horse . . . with someone seated on the horse. It had to be Mari! Another horse and rider trotted toward The Tree and unsaddled. Danni knew that was Jim. She ran to find Mr. Ahrens.

Kevin led his horse, with Mari seated astride it, to the headquarters building. He was dusty and pale, his blond hair straggling limply from beneath his now gray hat, as rivulets of sweat glazed his face. He pulled his gloves from his hands and slapped them hard against his dirt encrusted chaps. Two spots of high color flamed in his cheeks. Mari was withdrawn and silent as Lee helped her down from the horse.

Danni took a hesitant step toward Kevin as he turned to lead his horse to The Tree.

"I'll take care of her, if you want," she offered, sensing Kevin's tiredness.

He looked at her with dust-reddened eyes. "I'd appreciate it," he responded simply, and handed her the reins. Danni took her time and rubbed down the tired mare. When she returned to the cafeteria, Kevin sat on the porch with scrubbed face and hands, sipping a glass of ice water.

"Are you going to eat?" Danni asked, sitting opposite him.

"In awhile," Kevin responded shortly, staring out at the meadow. Danni looked at him for a moment.

"You seem kinda ticked off," she commented.

"Sorry, not with you." He turned and looked at her for the first time. "I should've known she'd do something like this. I should've gotten her off first. She has no idea how God took care of us out there. Other horses could have followed her, people could have gotten hurt. I could just—" he made a frustrated face.

"Well, you did really well with her," Danni consoled him. "Where did you catch up with her?"

"Down past Cowboy Camp!" Kevin sputtered indignantly. "She was *jumping*, of course, and her horse came down too fast. I caught her off balance and pulled her off. I was so mad I had to run back to camp talking to the Lord so I wouldn't say anything to her I shouldn't."

"You *ran* all the way back here?" Danni looked incredulous. "That's over two miles!"

"I had to," Kevin said, a sheepish grin finally softening his face. "You don't know how mad I was."

Although she tried not to, Danni felt laughter bubbling up inside of her. She bit her lips, put her head down, snickered, then finally laughed out loud. She peeked up at Kevin and saw him smiling down at her, shaking his head in mock dismay.

"Sorry, Kevin," she finally managed. "I'm just imagining you gritting your teeth and running all the way back up the meadow. You are so good! I would've given her an earful."

Kevin shrugged. "So much for me having her under control, huh? I wonder if Ahrens will send her home."

"Oh, poor thing," Danni groaned, wiping tears of mirth from her eyes. "Two summers and she hasn't made it through a whole week here yet!"

It turned out that Mari did not get sent home. Instead, she was allowed to stay at camp but was banned from riding any horses for the remainder of the week. She was also required to clean tack—saddles, bridles, and halters—for two hours a day, every day, until Friday.

"Do you think she's learned a lesson from this?" Danni asked Kevin and Jim later that evening over a meal of baked potatoes and salad.

Kevin made a rude noise. Jim just shook his head. "You can't tell with kids like Mari. She may never do anything like that again, or she may be planning for next time." He stretched his long arms above his head and yawned. "Do you think Eva will mind if I give campfire a miss tonight?" he asked at the end of his yawn. "This day has been a little too exciting, and I think I hear my bunk calling to me."

Danni chewed her lip for a moment before answering. "Why don't you both just take off for the evening? We're not even going to miss you, and I'm sure Mr. Ahrens will accept your absence."

"Don't let word get around that you can excuse people from activities," Jim warned her. "Methinks that you might suddenly find yourself with several new best friends."

"Don't worry," Danni laughed. "I don't think I can excuse people from anything! I just know that Eva won't mind, because she's already mentioned that you guys might like some extra sleep. You'd better go! If you don't, someone else may find something for you to do."

Jim jumped up agilely from the table, tray in hand, and vanished. Kevin lingered for a moment.

"Thanks, Danni. I think I could use some time just to vegetate." He paused as if he were going to say more, then bent to give her a one-armed hug. Danni returned his hug enthusiastically.

"I'm just glad you're OK," she told him. "Get some sleep."

June 27

The Quiet Hour

Dear People,

I am so tired! I've enjoyed this week, but I'm glad it's about over. I'm cabin sitting for Terri and Jenny so they can take a breather. Most of these girls are out cold. All of the walking/running around they do here really wears them out. I would go to sleep too, but Mari is awake, and I feel uneasy just shutting my eyes. She is sitting on her bunk glaring into space. I don't think that I was her first choice for being here. Then again, I wonder who would be.

Mari has been doing her free labor for the Horsemanship guys, and today is her last day. Lee tells me that she actually hasn't said much since her little adventure—in fact, she has stopped talking altogether lately. Kev feels kind of bad about it, since he thinks it might be because he didn't talk to her all the way back to camp that day, so he's taken to tipping his hat to her when she comes down to work, and saying "thanks" when she goes. He said he can't think of anything else to say to her. (That's Kevin!)

I found out that the camp store is selling the postcard design that I drew last summer! I am so excited! I have to send a postcard to Nana and Papa just so they can see it!

I got a note in my box on a green marbled piece of paper. It had salt water taffy taped to it. It was great! The funny thing was that all the note said was "John 15:5." Of course I looked it up. It said, "Without Me, you can do nothing." It was a reminder of our discussion in our PowerPack last Sunday. We talked about freedom of choice, and how God never tells us we can't do something—He lets us choose our way, and then when we're all messed up He fixes everything if we let Him. It's hard to understand that God does everything for us . . . even when we mess up. It would be easier if we didn't have the choice to do anything bad! Sometimes I just wish someone would write out all of the rules of everything right, and then I could do them all! If someone would just tell me what the right thing to do is, life would be so much easier.

I'm looking forward to seeing you guys on Monday. Bart, just bring your books with you—I want you to be here for the whole week. Maybe you and Gloria can study together. She's taking her boards the week after Family Camp. She has to wait six miserable weeks for the results.

I can't wait to see you! I'd better go, though. Mari just got up for some reason. Oh, she's going to the bathroom. Bye anyway.

Love you all—

Danni

It was too early when the buses came. It seemed as if Danni had never gone to bed—she had put away the Saturday night program props in the storage room, closed her eyes for a few seconds, and then it was 5:00 a.m.

The general staff members were singing loudly as they unloaded truckload after truckload of camper suitcases and sleeping bags. Danni got into the generally zany spirit as she double-checked luggage tags and called out the bus lists. A feeling of ebullience bubbled just beneath the surface of the staff. They had made it through the first week!

There were tearful good-byes between staff and campers. Lucretia and Lawanna waved good-bye and boarded the bus singing a new song that they had learned in Camp Council, "God Don't Make No Junk." Danni grinned as she thought of what parents would say about the song's bad grammar.

Independent Mari made her way slowly toward her bus, in plenty of time for once to get to where she needed to go. She paused for a moment before getting on and looked around her, scanning the faces of the staff and remaining campers to find someone.

Kevin was hauling the last of the luggage into a rear compartment of the bus and emerged just as Mari turned his way. Her face lit up and she struggled over to him.

"Kevin? I—I'm really sorry—for everything," she stuttered, her face pale and anxious with her need for his forgiveness.

Kevin, taken by surprise, pulled off his cap, then replaced it. He shoved his hands into his pockets. "Ah, Mari, that's OK," he replied. "I guess you won't do it again, right?" He pulled his hand out of his pocket and patted her awkwardly.

Mari threw her arms around his waist and hugged him as hard as she could. Then she turned away and pulled herself onto the bus. Kevin stood in stunned silence for a moment, then grinned.

"Bye, Mari!" he called after her. "See you next summer!"

He turned to Danni. "See? She's great. Didn't I tell you she was just like my little sister?"

Danni stuck her tongue out at him.

CHAPTER 5

Cowboys 'n' Indians

By Sunday night Danni knew that it was going to be a crazy week. Staff, released from the extra responsibility of campers, were pulling wild pranks on each other. The Cowboy staff had launched a full scale assault on the Native Village, complete with water guns and balloon grenades. The Villagers, supposedly preparing their settlement for a week of Family Camp visitors, instead plotted revenge. Jim had coaxed Gloria out to The Tree for some relaxation from studying, and had "cooled her off" with a dunk in the horse trough. Winona had stood by with her camera for photographic evidence. Even Mr. Ahrens was not safe. He entered his office to find it entirely rearranged, desk and all. Even the pictures were on opposite walls.

"Someone apparently does not have enough to do," Mr. Ahrens said good-naturedly. "I will find out who did this, and then they are *mine*," he added darkly. Danni didn't even dare crack a smile. She had a feeling that she knew who had done it. Her suspicion had been stirred early that afternoon when she saw Perry coming down from the third floor of the main lodge, whistling innocently.

"Can't chat now—late to work," he told her as he

breezed by. Later that night Danni heard an outraged yelp from down the hall.

"Who short-sheeted my bed? You guys are in for it!" Darren Irwin closed his door with a thump.

Perry was busy that week. Between putting bags of frozen peas in Eva's bed and making a remarkably real looking dummy out of some of the props in the program room, he served excellent meals in the cafeteria and endeared himself to the Family Campers. Perry's mother and his brother, Joel, joined the campers on Monday. They had no idea about his extracurricular activities.

"Are you getting any rest here?" Mrs. Bowman asked worriedly as she surveyed the busy dining room at lunch that day.

"Oh, sure, Mom," Perry looked at her earnestly. "I sleep like a log every night."

Danni, overhearing, held her breath to smother a giggle.

"Where's Bart?" Squatting next to her father, with her clipboard clutched to her chest, Danni pushed back her earphones to receive his reply.

Her father shook his head. "In the cabin, probably. He's really very serious about his classes this summer, and he studies every chance he can get."

"Oh." Danni felt deflated. "Well, can you make sure that he comes to the program tomorrow? It's Eva's day off, and I'm running everything myself. I want him to see what I do."

Her father squeezed her shoulder with a work-roughened hand. "I'll see what I can do, Danni-dee," he promised her solemnly.

The Mallory family enjoyed a full day on Wednesday. Betti and Dad competed at archery, Betti coming away with a trophy balloon for her efforts; Bart finally took a break to take a few turns around the Go-cart track with his father. Danni caught glimpses of her family throughout the day as she busily planned for her special campfire event.

Tuesday and Wednesday night campfires were in some ways the easiest campfires of the week. Family Campers got to choose which outpost campsite they would visit for the night, whether it be the Native Village, the Frontierland, or the Cowboy Camp. Each camp had its own program set up, complete with guitarists and song leaders, game leaders and storytellers. All Danni had to do was make sure that each camp had their props and knew exactly what they were doing.

"Why don't you come up to the Village tonight when you've gotten everybody set up?" asked Jay Dunstan, waylaying Danni on her way to the Headquarters building. "I could use you in a skit we're doing."

"Skit? What skit?" Danni eyed him quizzically. "I thought you had all of your people."

"I do, I do," Jay hastened to explain. "You wouldn't have to say anything, I would just be using you as an example of a prisoner in a native village."

"You're going to scalp me, then?" Danni asked with an easy laugh.

Jay smiled his deep, dimpled smile. "Not exactly," he hedged. "Just burn you at the stake."

"Great," Danni agreed sarcastically. "I'll be there."

"You will?" Jay looked at her with hopeful eyes.

"Of course! Anything for the arts," Danni joked, hurrying on her way.

Danni carefully parted and braided her hair for her role. Tying the ends of her braids with strips of leather, she stood back and critically examined the effect.

"Not bad," Winona grunted, digging her cowboy boots out from the footlocker under her bed. She smoothed her hair down and put on a small black Stetson, remarkably similar to Kevin's.

Danni turned from the mirror. "You're wearing *that* to the Native Village?" she asked incredulously. "Be careful, my dear. Don't forget they're on the warpath up there."

"I'm not going to the Village," Nona said flatly, hemming her lips into a straight line.

"Oh? But . . ." Danni knew when to stop asking questions.

It occurred to her then that something had gone wrong between Winona and Jay. Obviously, Winona, with her dark eyes and wealth of dark hair, would have been a natural for any role of a native prisoner that Jay would need. Danni was a late understudy for her part.

"Is . . . is there something wrong? Do you need to talk?" asked Danni timidly.

"Nope." Winona shook her head. "See ya." She closed the door firmly.

Danni felt a jolt run through her. She suddenly wished very, very much that Eva was around. All at once, running things on her own seemed a much more nerve-racking prospect than it had that morning. Danni opened the door to leave, and uttered a brief prayer.

"Lord, I want to do the right thing," Danni whispered as she started down the quiet hall. "I don't want to be in the middle of whatever trouble there is. Please help me see what I should do."

A truckload of noisy staff members stopped and drove Danni up the steep hill to the Native Village and Frontierland. She almost had declined the ride, but accepted on the basis that she had to be reasonable—she didn't drive, and she had to get around quickly tonight of all nights.

When she arrived at the Native Village the program was well underway. Indian wrestling games and contests of skill in archery had the campers busily involved. Mike Hoyt, one of Jay's less-than-willing volunteers, supervised a game in which contestants stood in a circle and slapped each other's open palms. Anyone who stepped out of the circle or moved their feet, lost.

"Dannielle, your hair looks so wonderful." Betti, seated on a stump stool beamed at her stepdaughter.

"You were right about that flaming arrow bit," her dad joked as he put his arm around her waist. "Took years off my life, but made a nice start to the show." He lowered his voice and leaned in close to her ear. "With your hair like that, my Danni-dee, you look just like your mother did. Did you know that?" He smiled at her and the firelight showed in his shiny eyes.

Danni bit back pain. Her father only rarely spoke about her mother. She found herself reaching out for memories of her, and was dismayed to find that the sharp images were much fuzzier now.

"She would be so proud of you," her father continued.

Danni held his eyes and smiled. A twig snapped and Kat slipped out of the shadows behind one of the tepees ringing the blazing fire. She motioned for Danni to come.

"Pssst! Danni! Where have you been? I've been looking all over for you!" Kat's iron grip dragged Danni back into the gloom.

"What do you want?" Danni asked, knowing she sounded short, but not caring.

Kat looked at her oddly. "Nothing. Jay says to get into costume."

"Oh." Danni slipped off her sweatshirt and pulled the brown, fringed felt dress over her T-shirt and shorts.

"Great," Kat encouraged her. "Slip on some moccasins and you'll look authentic. I'm so glad you agreed to this. I told Jay you'd look loads better in this than Nona."

Danni felt a jolt of discomfort.

"So, Nona was supposed to do this?" she asked uneasily.

Kat gave her a sharp look. "Of course not. Everyone knows Nona and Jay aren't getting along right now."

Danni pressed forward. "But did anyone ask her?"

"She ducked out—and why is this an issue?" Kat demanded, sounding more like her usual self.

Danni was at a loss for words. She looked for a long moment at Kat, who met her gaze boldly. Finally Danni found her voice.

"Winona really likes you, and I know Jay thinks you're a great person," Danni began slowly.

"What's your point?" Kat's voice was belligerent.

"I think you should . . . respect that, OK? Don't take advantage of the situation." Danni felt the words bubble from her.

"I haven't done anything to Jay," Kat blurted in a furious, low voice. "It's none of your business, and I don't want to talk about it with you." She pulled Danni toward the firelight. "Come on."

Danni played her part without incident, and perhaps better than she had hoped to. As she was tied to the stake, a small black spider crawled from the stake to her shoulder. Her panic was no act. As soon as the skit was over and she was released, she shook the creature off and shuddered.

"Why does this type of thing always seem to happen to me?" she complained to her brother, Bart, on the way down the dark trail toward the base camp. Their parents had opted out of hiking the half mile in total darkness and had taken a shuttle van instead.

"Just your luck to be there, Poccahontas," her brother teased her.

"Seriously, Bart, I don't know what to say to Winona. Should I say anything? I mean, I don't want her to know that Kat's trying to get Jay's attention, but shouldn't she know that the good friend who helps her out all that time—whom she *trusts*, Bart, is stabbing her in the back? I just want to do the right thing!"

Bart shrugged enigmatically. "I don't know, baby sister. I'm not up on all this male-female stuff."

Danni sputtered. "That's an incredible lie, and you know it," she insisted. "Don't you even have an opinion on this at all?"

"Some things have to just work themselves out, Danni," Bart responded. "Sometimes the right thing is to do nothing. Your best bet is to go put away your props and go to bed. That's where I'm off to."

He gave her a hug as they reached the end of the trail, and scrubbed his knuckles across her hair.

"Stop it, you ape!" Giggling, she twisted out of his grasp and punched his arm.

"Ape, am I? Ape?" Bart began to shadow box around her, his feet shuffling comically.

"Wait . . .wait. I have to ask you something serious. Bart, stop."

His boxing slowed, then halted. "What now?" he asked.

She looked over his shoulder at the road. "Do you remember what Mama looked like?"

"Whoa," Bart said quietly. "That came out of nowhere." He dropped his arms and shoved his hands into his pockets.

"Do you?" Danni persisted.

Bart stood for a moment and thought. "Yeah. It's been a long time since I tried to picture her, though. I wasn't around that much when she was . . . you know, sick.

"Yeah," Danni said. They stood for a moment without talking. "Well, thanks," she shrugged. "I just wanted to know just . . . because, you know?"

Bart nodded and pulled her into a hug. They stood for awhile and just breathed the same air. Then the hug got tighter and Danni started smothering, and she let out a little squeak and started battering her brother all over his back and shoulders.

"That's what I get for giving my baby sister a little affection. Women these days . . ." Bart started off at a jog for the cabin area. Danni watched him go with a warmth inside. They had never before been able to talk about their mother. She was grateful.

She stood in the quiet blackness for awhile, looking up at the stars above the Lupine House and the Lupine Meadow Lodge a few yards away. Problems with her roommate seemed small in the face of so many faraway heavenly bodies. For the first time that evening she felt at peace. She breathed it in, until the crackle of twigs in the darkness startled her from her reverie.

"Who's side are you on? Are you a Cowboy or a Native?" a muffled voice inquired.

Brought back down to earth, Danni snapped, "I'm not on anybody's side. I am the assistant program director, and if you try to involve me in this, you will be very, very sorry. Good night!"

She turned on her heel and stalked away.

Later she heard that the Natives, led by a red-haired squaw named Black Swan and a brave chief named Autumn Fox, led an incredible counter attack against the Cowboys and, catching them off guard, stole several of their horses and a utility truck. Danni noted that she didn't care.

On her day off she found that her odd mood persisted. Winona had been uncharacteristically silent in the room the night before, and was gone before worship the following morning. Danni had found a note from Jay on the door, and was surprised to see that it was addressed to her. He had thanked her for making the campfire a success and hoped that she would come up and visit when she had time. Danni felt a flood of sympathy when she realized that there was no note for Winona. Unfortunately, she had no opportunity to talk to her roommate, and could find no one who knew where she was shooting film for the day. Frustrated and out of sorts, she asked her parents to drive her to Carterville, the nearest town, for lunch and a short shopping trip.

Betti laid down her dishtowel, surprised. "Danni, don't you want to go up to the arts and crafts building and work on a project today?"

Her father laughed. "Betti, she's got all summer to be here. She's probably feeling a little cooped up, that's all—isn't that right, Danni-dee?" He patted her shoulder lovingly.

Danni could hear her voice sounding much like Kat's. "I need to get out of here."

All three Mallorys turned and stared at her. Bart dropped his jaw comically.

"Is this still my sister?" he teased. She glowered at him.

"Dannielle, is everything all right?" Her father's green eyes studied her.

Danni felt like screaming and bolting out of the cabin, but she realized that this would solve nothing. Her irritation was with herself, with Kat, with Nona and Jay. Her family had nothing to do with it.

"Daddy, Betti," she heard herself say with strained calmness, "I really need to get away for awhile. I promise to explain what's going on later, but please, can we just go now?"

"No problem, princess." Mr. Mallory fished his car

keys out of a suitcase pocket. "Your wish is our command, isn't that right, Bart?" He piloted his son toward the cabin door.

"I have to *shop?*" Bart groaned.

"Sometimes retail therapy is all that will work," Betti teased him, grabbing her purse.

Danni had time to sort her feelings out as she spent the afternoon with her family. The frustration inside of her eased, and the knot of anger that had given her a dull headache all day finally dissolved and dissipated. "Retail therapy," as Betti so jokingly put it, also gained her a new pair of hiking boots, a denim "skort," and a thick, cloth-bound journal. She considered buying something for Kevin, then dismissed the idea, being unable to find anything not too personal but personal enough.

"Are you feeling better *yet?*" Bart whined at the salad bar of the restaurant they lunched at.

Danni laughed out loud. "Thank you for your overwhelming sympathy, you oaf. I'm fine now."

"Really? Can we quit?" He raised quizzical brows at her.

"Yes, we're done," she relented.

"Have you figured out what you're going to do?" he asked.

"Nope." Danni shrugged and stuck a celery stalk in her mouth. She crunched cheerfully for a moment.

"A wise person told me once that some things just had to work themselves out, and I guess that's what I'm going to do." She swallowed and blotted her mouth daintily with a napkin. "I think that's the right thing to do."

"Good call." Bart gave her a light punch, and they rejoined their parents.

Danni's decision to leave well enough alone did not prepare her for the sight that greeted her when she returned to her room after lunch. Betti was with her, carrying a bag of plums she had purchased at a roadside stand. They stared in amazement at the disordered room. An open bag lay half packed on Nona's bed. The footlocker, which usually was hidden, was pulled out from beneath the bed. Winona herself froze with an armload of clothes.

"What are you doing?" Danni all but shouted, just as Winona commented, "You're back!"

Both girls stared at each other for a moment. Decisively, Danni strode the rest of the way into the room, and pulled Betti with her. She plopped down onto her bed.

"Winona, what's up?" she asked. "What's going on?"

"Should I leave?" Betti asked, half standing.

"Yes," decided Danni.

"No!" exclaimed Winona.

Betti stood and shook her head. "Winona, I'm Betti, Danni's stepmother. I think we should all sit down and talk for a bit. Here." She took the clothes from Nona's arms and set them on top of the footlocker. She guided Winona to a spot on her bed and pushed her down gently. Then she stood away from the two girls, leaning against the closed door.

Silence hung for a moment, then Danni spoke in a low voice. "Are you leaving?"

Winona shook her head. "It's no big deal—I was going to leave you a note about it. I know I've been disturbing you with getting up so early. I thought I'd just move down to the general staff quarters so that I could come and go without bothering anyone. I really was going to leave you a note."

Danni felt that she was out of breath. "Don't you think I'd tell you if you were bothering me? You never bother me. This has been working out fine." She was silent. "I don't think that's what this is about."

Winona sat for a moment, seeming to sink inside of herself. Danni said, "We missed you up at the Native Village last night. You really should have been part of the program there."

Nona didn't raise her eyes. "There's all kinds of stuff there that I don't think I'm a part of," she replied shortly, weaving her fingers together in her lap. It seemed to take an effort for her to sit still.

"I don't know what you mean," Danni leaned forward, eyes pleading. "I don't even know what's going on, except that at the last minute Jay asked me to be in a skit."

"And you couldn't *wait* to get up there and help him out."

"It's not like that!" Danni replied, stung. "I was help-ing him out, but don't you think that's part of my job? He said he needed someone extra for a skit. If you want to find someone to be suspicious of, you should really talk to—" Danni stopped herself with an effort. She was angry with herself and with Winona for causing the scene.

"Kat, right? I know your opinion of her. I guess it doesn't matter that you helped Jay out, Danni. I just feel . . ." She blew out a breath. "This has been such a weird summer. So much has gone on, and I feel like . . . well, never mind. I apologize. None of this is your fault."

Danni shrugged, feeling confused. "I'm sorry that it bothered you so much that I helped Jay. I really don't want to lose a friend over something like this."

Nona shrugged. She pushed an armload of clothes aside and stood. "I knew I should have worked at the Native Village. I've felt Jay drifting away from me all summer . . . I'm sorry I took it out on you. None of this is your fault."

"I'm just glad you're staying," Danni said simply.

"Well, I'd better start putting this mess away . . ."

Nona sighed and gathered her clothes.

Neither girl noticed that Betti had slipped out quietly.

July 6

Hey you guys,

Thank you so much for everything. Every time you leave, I wish you could stay a little bit longer. I really miss you already.

The Native Village and the Cowboys have been hammering out a peace treaty since Saturday night. The raids got a little bit out of hand; some of the Natives were caught behind enemy lines and "branded" with the 'Lazy L' brand—in fluorescent, indelible ink. Mr. A thought that was a little much, especially since the Natives' revenge included inverted mohawks for some unlucky victims. The little pranks, though, are still going on. I got my first dose of the horse trough at The Tree right after you guys left. I guess Kevin didn't want me to feel homesick.

Winona and I are still walking on eggshells with each other, but at least she's not going anywhere. I hope that she's trusting Kat Armstrong a little less, but I doubt it. She and Jay have not patched things up. Winona says that maybe it was just time, and that someday I'll understand that. I don't dare even comment on that.

I wish that this had never happened—for obvious reasons. Eva and I have decided to switch off doing outpost campfires for a few weeks. She'll cover the smaller campfires for Tuesday and Wednesday at Frontierland and the Native Village while I'll go down to Cowboy. I hope that helps things. We'll see. Pray for Gloria! She is taking her boards this week. She is so stressed! Pray for Perry to get better, too.

Betti, I keep trying to write in my journal, but I can't think of anything positive to say yet!

Take care, you guys. I love you.

Danni

CHAPTER 6

Innocent Little Lambs

"One of the best things about Cub Camp," Tina said cheerfully as she stacked clean cups next to the juice and milk dispensers in the dining room, "is that these kids don't eat much. You can give 'em a PB&J sandwich and they're raring to go again."

Jenny, who was subcounseling for the week, rolled her eyes as she scraped food off of trays into the trash can.

"Obviously you've never had a cabin during Cub Week," she chuckled. "If you can get these kids to eat anything at all you're doing great. I have never seen so many kids who eat only a bite or two!" She thumped a tray down for emphasis.

Christine Porter, who was a counselor at the Cowboy Camp, added her two cents as she passed by. "I'd rather have a cabin of the most difficult disABILITY kids in the world than have Cub kids," she said, wrinkling her nose. "Have fun this week, girls." She waved as she caught up with her wagon unit.

"Little kids really give me the creeps," Mike Hoyt put in as he stopped to refill his juice glass. "I'd rather work general staff any day than put up with the three W's—wiggling, whining, and wetting. I have a little sister at home."

"I don't know," Darla shook her head as she dumped

the garbage from her tray. "I plan to enjoy all of this. My mom was always acting like we were so horrible when we were little. I think this'll be fun! I mean, how bad can little kids be?"

"Shyanne . . . Shyanne, I'm tired. Can't we take a rest?" whined a small pigtailed miss with a smudged face. Shyanne paused in ascending the incline toward the nature center. "Rochelle, you can walk 10 more feet and stop for a minute in the shade. If you keep stopping on the road you'll never get to the waterfall."

"Waterfall?" Her eyes brightened. "What waterfall?" She trotted willingly up the hill.

Charlie Rhoades gave Shyanne a big grin as she and her charge came up the hill. They were the last to join the group.

"There you all are," Bill said heartily, and started his spiel about the rules of the nature center and what they would see today. As soon as he could get close enough to her, Charlie said in a low voice to Shy, "How's it going so far?"

"Just great," she whispered back. "They need a little incentive to walk anywhere far, but other than that, they're OK."

"Mine are great with walking," Charlie admitted, "but how do I get them to quit? They want to just run off everywhere in eight different directions! I don't know if I can do this." He broke off quickly and separated two of his boys who had begun to trip each other. Shyanne surveyed her brood, still listening attentively. She fought down a feeling of superiority.

"Just don't forget what Darren said," Shyanne reminded Charlie in a whisper. "As long as you give the appearance of being in control, they'll believe it. You can do it."

"I hope so," muttered Charlie, raking his fingers

through his coppery hair. He jammed his hands in his pockets and tried to look "in control."

"Oh, this has got to be the heaviest week of the summer," moaned Esther Marshall, who was filling in for Gloria and running the office in Headquarters. "I have had more little ones in here with invisible splinters, microscopic knee scrapes, and stomachaches than I care to remember."

"Keep up the good work," Marge Ahrens reassured her. "Just continue to pass out Band-Aids and hugs, and they'll all be fine."

"I just hope nothing serious comes through before Gloria gets back," Esther shuddered. "I know only how to give shots. I haven't had much nursing lab past that."

"Don't worry," Marge soothed her. "Steve, up at Frontierland, is an EMT during the winter. If we need him he's only a radio call away."

"Unless he's on an overnighter," muttered Esther, who was not known for her optimism.

"Well, it's a pajama party week," yawned Eva who had stayed up late to drill Gloria one last time before she drove back to Lakeland for her boards.

"I know you're sleepy, but I don't think little kids sleep," laughed Danni who was searching through the prop closet for something to dress a big bad wolf in.

"No, seriously—it's a pajama party week. Sometime during this week we should have a pajama party for the kids."

"Is that like a teddy bear picnic?" Danni studied Eva to gauge her seriousness.

"Not exactly, although they can bring a stuffed animal if they want to. We just show an old kids' movie one night in the campfire bowl, and have all of the kids come down in pajamas—with their coats on and blankets and stuff. We have hot popcorn and hot chocolate, and build up the fire to keep them warm."

"Maybe we'd better hold off on the drinks after 6:00, or at least limit them to one each," Danni reminded Eva wryly, and Eva grimaced.

"OK—forgot about the bed accidents. We could just have popcorn."

"Naah, let's do the chocolate too. So, we're doing this Thursday night?"

"Yeah. That'll work." Eva yawned hugely and laid her head on her desk. "Are we all ready for tonight?" her voice was muffled.

"Yep—the pool people are clowns tonight, and they're coming in for makeup at 6:00. I will have the costumes patched by then. Everybody else is support staff with Tim down on the baseball field for relay games. The band will be set up by 6:00 and general staff is taking care of the set up and take down. Ahrens already picked the band music, and the peanuts and apple juice are being bagged by the kitchen kids as we speak." Danni took a breath after her lengthy recitation.

"Oh, good." Eva kept her head down on her arms. For a moment, Danni thought she was asleep. She was ready to move quietly into the prop room when Eva lifted up her head.

"Do you know what? I don't know what I'd do without you. You're great." She pushed away from her desk and stood up. "Let's go take a break and see if Perry is back from delivering breakfast to the Outpost camps. Maybe he'll give us some Popsicles." She looped an arm around Danni's waist and dragged her toward the door.

Perry was not in the kitchen when Eva and Danni arrived, but Carlotta, one of the cooks, had a soft spot in her heart for the staff. She came up with fruit-flavored frozen pops for both girls, then she shooed them out onto the cafeteria porch. As they finished the cold, sweet treat, Eva admitted that she was finally going to give in to her yawns and sleep the remaining two hours until lunch. Danni decided to do the costume patching on the clown outfits in her room. She left a note on the office door, gathered the costumes, and climbed the three flights of stairs to the room she and Winona shared.

On a whim, she approached Darren Irwin's door and tapped on it.

"It's open," Perry coughed. Danni pushed open the door and peeped into the bare room. Perry was lying on his back in Darren's spare bed. His arm was flung over his face. He removed it.

"Are you sleeping, or what?" Danni averted her startled gaze from his red-rimmed eyes.

"Hang out," Perry invited cheerfully. "I'm just here feeling sorry for myself."

"What for?" Danni sat cross-legged in the doorway.

"Ah, it's nothing. I'll tell you my problem if you tell me yours." He raised his brows. "What's up with you?"

Danni made a noise and shook her head. "This hasn't been the easiest week." She found herself pouring out the story of Kat and Winona and Jay to Perry's sympathetic ears. She was startled to hear herself add, "It just seems like this is all my fault. If I had just spoken up and really laid it on the line to Kat, this would never have happened. I'm just too big of a wimp to ever really do or say anything I really feel." She lifted her eyes from the button she was replacing, and saw Perry nodding his head in agreement.

"Hey, wait a minute. You're not supposed to agree," she protested jokingly.

"Yeah, I am. Do you want truth or not? Sometimes you *are* a wimp. Kat ran over you all last summer. She said just whatever she wanted to, and you ducked as though you deserved it. You always think everything is your fault." He cleared his throat and shifted up onto his elbow. "You should've told her where she could go a long time ago, Danni. You just cave in at the weirdest times. You always want to do the 'right' thing, and sometimes you end up not doing anything at all . . . and that doesn't work either!"

Nettled, Danni jabbed her needle through the tiny hole in the button. Wasn't he full of criticism suddenly! "Well, there's something to be said for Christlike behavior," she began firmly, but Perry cut her off.

"Aw, man. See? Even now you could have just said, 'Perry, it's none of your business,' or, 'lay off.' You know you want to. Instead, you just go all righteous and condemning on everyone. That quiet guilt stuff really stinks. That's what comes of trying to be right. You end up trying to look better than everybody else. Why don't you just speak your mind, instead? I'm not saying you should go crazy with it and be shooting off all the time on people, but man, Danni, life's too short to—" He cut off abruptly, shaking his head.

Danni looked up from snapping off a length of thread. "To what?"

"Nothing. I'm wasting my breath. Lecture's over," Perry mumbled from behind his arm again.

"Are you OK?" Danni asked cautiously.

"Just fine," Perry muttered.

Danni took a deep breath. "OK, Perry, now I'm not going to be a wimp. I'm speaking my mind. I got a look at you and you look like you're really in the dumps about something, and I know that we get on each other's nerves sometimes but we *are* friends, and I know that talking about it would probably help—and you said you would." She finished her big speech.

Perry was lying on his side, laughing silently. Danni pursed her lips in irritation.

"Why is that funny?" she demanded, hearing her voice get snippy.

Perry sat up and swung his legs over the edge of the bed. He slid down to sit on the floor. He sighed. "I'm sorry, Danni. It's just that there you go again. You just don't understand that you can't always fix everybody's problems. Remember last summer? When Eva and David were having a falling out? You schemed and planned and got mad at me when I told you to leave well enough alone. Your brother gave you the right advice—just let the Jay and Winona thing work itself out. Then they'll be fine, and as soon as I take a nap, I'll be fine too."

With her cheeks stinging, Danni gathered up her sewing. "I guess I'll go to my room," she muttered.

"You're being polite and 'right' again," Perry called as she was closing the door. "Somebody had to tell you this sometime, so don't go away mad."

"Don't go away mad, nothing," Danni kicked the door shut savagely behind her. The slam echoed throughout the short corridor, and she hoped that it kept Perry awake with remorse. She doubted it.

She sewed rough stitches in the next outfit, not really caring whether they were even or her seam was straight. She was heartily tired of being thought of as naive, too young, or not mature enough to understand that everything in life could not be fixed with a wink and a smile. First Kat, then Nona, and now Perry had all but shoved her face into the fact that she was an immature little girl. She angrily snapped a length of thread with her teeth. She didn't know why she cared what Perry thought anyway. He was just being a big shot because he was in charge of the Outpost Camp's meals, and got to drive out and deliver them, then drive back to pick up their empty dishes.

Danni dug through her top drawer and pulled out her empty journal. She pulled an ink pen from the jar on her desk and wrote the date at the top of the page. Then she wrote: "Why do I have to even know Perry Bowman? He is such a jerk!"

It was immature, but it made Danni feel better—though it did nothing to erase the echo in her ears of what Perry had actually said.

Danni did not have much time to stew in her mood that week. Gloria returned on Tuesday, looking limply exhausted but relieved. Danni's days grew busy as she organized camp councils, attended staff meetings, and planned campfires. Perry smiled at her whenever he saw her, but she turned a blind eye toward him. She thought he looked too amused.

Wednesday night the Cowboy Campfire was a raving success. The campers listened spellbound to another exciting story from Cowboy Clint, one of the wranglers with a short, muscular build, gingery cropped hair, and a squidzillion freckles on his face. Clint Dunn was one of the best loved members of the Cowboy staff. Eddie, Russell, Clint, and Veronica made up the quartet of hardworking wranglers who were permanently assigned to the Cowboy Camp for the care of the horses there. Doug Pace, Eddie's older brother, was the Cowboy Camp director. This Wednesday was his day off.

"How'd ya like the special effects that time?" Danni overheard Clint ask Russell Ward as the campers drifted back onto the road for the hike back to their camps.

"Ah, that was great. Did you see everybody jump? It sounds just like a real gun."

Clint's response was muffled by a child's squeal in the darkness, but Russell's response was plain. "Really? That's so cool, man."

Danni frowned and turned toward the boys but they were soon lost to the darkness. She filed the conversation away in her mind for later.

It didn't much matter that there was a nip in the air, or that her blue, racing-back bathing suit was still a bit damp and cold from the night before. The moment the sun spilled liquid gold over the glassy lake Roseanne was up and out of her sleeping bag. She struggled into her clammy suit and brushed the sleep from her eyes. Down by the shore she could already see movement. Tommy Hayes, the other boat driver and the assistant director of the Waves program, was wading out into the water. Roseanne's fingers stuttered over her wet suit zipper. She had to get down to the boat before anyone else got there.

It was her own personal record—two weeks in a row. Two of the most glorious weeks of having the gorgeous Tommy to herself early in the morning. She sighed dreamily. A job on the water, working with a man like Tommy Hayes—it hardly seemed like work at all. She sighed again. If only she believed that. The truth was, the reason that she was skiing so early was not that she was chasing Tommy, or that she was attracted to the smooth-as-glass lake—which was a definite bonus. She had to ski early to get to ski at all.

"That's the breaks," Alan Weiss, the Waves director, told her sympathetically. "We have only two drivers out at a time, on two boats. You can ski early and late, but when we're teaching technique and doing practice runs we'll need you behind the wheel."

"No problem," Roseanne had hastened to assure him. What did he think, that she had come to camp just to play? She had known that she would be working. She just hadn't known how hard . . .

"Mornin'." Tommy smiled at her and tossed back his

sun-bleached hair as she reached the boat. She looked away from his too-perfect face. Perfect white teeth. Deep, expressive brown eyes and a deep, dark tan. Perfect dark blond hair. Even his eyelashes had been tipped blond by excessive sun exposure. And he was smiling at only her! (Of course, it did help that she was the only one there.)

She lugged herself into the boat, praying that she looked nimble and wide awake. "Ready to go?" She expected his usual response, and braced herself to the loud engine breaking the relative stillness of the morning.

"Um . . ." he turned and scanned the shore. From far away Roseanne could see the tarped shelter under which she and the other girls had slept. It looked as if none of the campers or staff had yet stirred. Roseanne followed Tommy's eyes with a feeling of dread.

"You're waiting for someone?" she asked feebly. (*Duh!* she chastised herself. *No, he's looking for wildlife. Can't you ask an intelligent question?*)

"Just Krista," he muttered, and gave that camp a last glance. "She said she never gets to see me otherwise." He started the engine.

"Krista?" Rosey gave him a surprised glance. Usually their other passenger was Cherrie, the camp cook. Her vivacious manner made the trip a treat—unless your sole aim was to spend time with Tommy Hayes alone. Then her presence was dreadful. Once or twice Alfred, a boy Roseanne had known forever, came out to practice his barefooting. Roseanne had been astonished to see his lanky frame turn into a powerful, graceful machine, fully in tune with the water. Krista was a soft-spoken girl who had a dry sense of humor that could surprise you. She was a good, fair counselor, but mostly she kept busy with her girls. Rosey would hardly have thought that Tommy would have even noticed her. Now it seemed that he had, and Rosey's time was about to be taken again.

"Well, maybe she overslept," she offered lamely. "I didn't hear anyone moving when I left."

"Maybe," shrugged Tommy, and steered the boat toward the south side of the lake. "I'm not gonna worry about it."

Roseanne felt like she was flying over the flat surface of the lake. The sky was filled with a few wisps of clouds that were stained a deep orange, then lavender. Rosey floated, with the cold water arcing back behind her. Tommy drove carefully and quickly, giving her enough warning to jump the wake of the boat when he turned. He gave her some pointers on barefooting, then got out to show her what he meant. It was 6:30 when they turned back toward the shore.

Krista was waiting when they got back to camp. Roseanne had enjoyed the companionable silence she and Tommy had shared as they walked up the ridge together. Now she sighed with frustration and turned to look back at the water.

"Don't worry," Tommy clapped her lightly on the shoulder, "we'll get out again tonight." He loped over to meet Krista.

The two-week chain of mornings alone with Tommy was broken the following morning. Cherrie was back in all of her enthusiasm. She wanted to learn to barefoot as well, and was especially interested in watching Tommy show her the moves. Krista came out the following morning, and shouted out cheerful conversation to Tommy over the roar of the engine about mutual friends of theirs and what they were doing. Roseanne paid far too much attention to the boat and less to her footing. She wiped out so many times that she was beginning to wonder if she had forgotten how to ski at all. Krista made sympathetic noises and suggested that she get into the boat and take a breather. Krista took her turn, and made the turns and jumps with ease. Rosey felt like she was eating ground glass. Jealousy, like an uncomfortable wool sweater, scratched and poked her everywhere.

Alfred started to spend more time out on the water. He took turns driving for Tommy while Roseanne felt useless and silly. The guys had their guy talk to keep them busy. Finally Roseanne got tired of feeling like a fifth wheel and skipped one morning. Alfred was waiting for her at worship with an anxious expression in his hazel eyes.

"Did you sleep OK? Are you sick?" he fired the questions at her rapidly. "Tommy had Cherrie wanting to ski, so he couldn't really wait. Did you oversleep? Are you mad?"

Roseanne laughed at him easily. "You guys don't need me to drive anymore. I thought I'd just sleep in for once."

"Oh. Well." Alfred stood for a moment, seeming at a loss for words. He cleared his throat. "I missed you."

"Thanks, Alfred! That's really sweet of you!" Roseanne gave him a one-armed hug. He seemed embarrassed.

"I mean it," he insisted, his open, boyish face a blotchy pink. "It wasn't the same without you."

Roseanne gave him a strange look and thanked him again. He crimsoned again from the roots of his curly dark hair and went away muttering about something he had to do.

"What I just want to know," Rosey wrote to Danni during The Quiet Hour, "is when is it going to be my turn? Here I do everything I can to spend time with Tommy—I go out there even when I'm totally exhausted so he'll have someone to drive for him. And what do I get? I wish sincerely that he'd make up his mind. At least I'd know if I was even in the running. I do know something now—I'm close to wishing that they'd all drown or get sunburn or go home or something. Even Alfred's in the way. I am so envious! Help!"

On Thursday night they broke camp and packed up their things to head for the Meadows. Once there, they would enjoy the activities that the base camp offered for the evening, then set out the following day for a lazy raft trip down the Braxley to close out the week. Roseanne always took Fridays off. This Friday, as she watched Cherrie, Krista, and the others go off, she was depressed. She made up her mind to forget all about Tommy. She dragged herself to the headquarters building, determined to read her mail, borrow the car from Kevin, and drown her sorrows in a Fenton's ice cream soda and a lonely matinee in Carterville.

She riffled through the mail in her box and pulled her fingers through her hair. She decided that she needed a trim, maybe even a dramatic cut. She mentally added that to her list of things to do in Carterville. "I'm gonna wash that man right outta' my hair," she sang to herself, then grinned sourly.

A thin sheet of paper with bold green writing on it stopped her on the way out of the door. It read:

"Dear Green-eyed Girl:

Did you know that Krista is his cousin?

One down and one to go!

Smile!

Danni"

Roseanne flew out of Headquarters toward the program room, shrieking like a siren.

"Daaaannnnniiiii!"

CHAPTER 7

Doing the Right Thing

Danni really never got to talk much to Eva before another week started. The next thing she knew, it was Sunday afternoon, the buses were coming in, and the gears of the week were churning again.

"It seems so strange that half of the staff will be gone most of the week," Danni complained, watching Roseanne stroll by with a group of older-looking campers. "I'm not sure that this Waves Camp is such a great idea."

"It's bringing a lot of older kids into the program," Eva reminded her. "What 15-or 16-year-old wouldn't just love to spend the entire week at the lake skiing? And a raft trip at the end of the week? I'd want to go."

"Yeah, I guess," Danni shrugged. "It's just that I hardly see Lena or Darla or Roseanne anymore, and now they're all out at Outpost camps. Guess it's time to make some new friends."

Eva frowned at the glum note in Danni's voice. "What's the matter, Dannielle? That doesn't sound like you."

Danni shrugged again. "I don't even know what *is* me," she complained bitterly. She recounted her conversation with Perry. "I don't think I try to prove that

I'm better than people, or try to fix things so that the only right way is my way. And I'm certainly not righteous or condemning," she concluded, scowling and shaking her head.

Eva lifted up her hands, palms up. "Everybody has a personality that's a little grating to others once in awhile," she admitted. "Maybe Perry was having a bad day."

"No, no—that's not the point," Danni heard her voice going up the scale as she fought for control. "I think Perry's *right*. I guess I am always 'right.' I always do the 'right' kinds of things. It's a habit I have—I try to figure out what everyone wants, and keep things nice. It's just the way I am—but," she choked out a laugh, "I like it. It doesn't hurt anyone, does it?"

Eva frowned uncertainly, clearly wanting not to involve herself. "If you like yourself, then what Perry said doesn't matter, does it, Danni?"

Danni sighed. "It's not supposed to. But what if everyone else sees that side of me too? What do you think, Eva? Do you think I'm self-righteous?"

Eva shook her head. "Danni, don't let this shake your self-confidence. You are who you are. You're my friend, and I appreciate what you've done for me. Perry needs our prayers and support—you know he is really going through a struggle right now."

Danni looked over curiously. "What's going on with him? I did notice that he looked a little bit down when I talked to him the other day."

Eva's expression was guarded. Her eyes looked deeply into Danni's, and she got the feeling that Eva was reading her mind. "He'll have to tell you that himself," she said finally, her brisk manner unusually gentle. "Just keep praying for him."

It was Wednesday before Danni knew it. Thursday

was her day off, and she was looking forward to taking it easy, maybe spending some time with Glenda or begging Kevin for an easy horseback ride through the pine-covered mountain trails. If she could make it through this last Outpost campfire, the night would speed by from there.

Danni packed a quick prop box with outfits for the Native Village campfire. Eva breezed into the office, carrying a stack of scripts in her arms and a pen in her teeth. She looked gratefully at Danni.

"Thanks—I am running so far behind!" Eva dumped the scripts on her desk and grabbed her jacket from the coathook. She took a moment to run a comb through her short, black hair.

"So, you're set for the programs at Frontierland and the Native Village?" Danni asked as she grabbed her clipboard and dug in her desk drawer for a pen.

"Yep," Eva replied around a mouthful of hairband. "It's going well. I just wish that they wouldn't do the wilderness food thing every week—but I guess that it's the kids' favorite part to see Steve eat that grasshopper."

Danni just shuddered and shook her head. "Whatever works, I guess."

Eva finished her hair. "Things going smoothly at Cowboy?"

"I think so," Danni shrugged. "The kids really love it, so I guess that's what counts, hm?"

"Yep—Cowboy's always a winner." Eva banged out the door with a quick good-bye.

Sitting on a fragrant hay bale in the circle of firelight, Danni felt a nagging something at the back of her mind. There was something she was forgetting to do—and then she remembered. Russell and Clint. The prop gun for the story. She looked cautiously around the circle of staff and campers. She had to grin as she saw Lee—or

Lyly, as she had finally permitted herself to be called—dwarfed by a huge cowboy hat and fancy boots. She spotted Russell playing the guitar for the songleader. Clint was to his right, being admired by a group of kids. Danni especially took note of a dark-haired boy who lit up whenever Clint spoke to him. Danni kept her eyes fixed on the two of them.

"Isn't that moon awesome?" Kevin plopped down on the bale next to Danni. She barely glanced at the full moon rising like a glowing stone above the black hills. She nodded at Kevin, and smiled vaguely.

"You OK?" he asked her.

"I'm fine," she replied, finding Clint with her eyes again.

As Clint's story began, Danni took a quick moment to glance around again. Russell was nowhere to be found. Frowning, Danni considered getting up, then relaxed when he materialized at the far side of the campfire. Clint's tale progressed. The story was about two brothers who fought a duel over something or other, but Danni found it hard to be interested.

Russell had heard his cue, for he leaned back and pulled a snub-nosed pistol from behind him. Holding it away from his body, he straightened his arm and held it steady. Danni concentrated on seeing the weapon in the darkness.

BOOM!

Campers jumped and squealed. Danni, despite the fact that she had heard the story at least three times before, found herself jerking involuntarily at the roar of sound. When she had recovered herself she decided that this was as good a time as any. She climbed over the hay bale she had been sitting on and found Russell in the dark. "May I see that gun, please?" she asked. Russell, in-tent on showing it to a handful or so of campers, had not heard her approach. He jumped a little.

"Oh, hi—Danni, right. Sure, you can see it." He handed her the weapon. She moved a little ways away from the campers to look at it.

"This is a real gun." It was not a question.

"Well, yeah." Russell raised his eyebrows, waiting.

"And it's loaded—you're using real bullets?" her voice was rising. Russell looked bewildered. "I guess . . ." His voice trailed off, and he looked up with relief as Clint approached.

"What's up, darlin'?" Clint's country twang and supremely casual manner offended Danni.

"I'm asking why you guys are using real guns and real bullets around the kids," Danni said, frowning slightly. "I know you take them on your overnighters for snakes and stuff, but . . ." She waited, arms hanging loosely at her sides. Clint looked at her, then gave a charming grin. "Uh, Russ, you can take five. I'll handle this." He winked at his friend, who stepped back toward the campfire.

"Now then." He turned back to Danni, taking the gun. "This is registered to me. Doug Pace knows I have it. There really isn't a problem with it, is there? I mean, it's only for the story."

"You know," she suggested, "we have prop guns you guys could use. Somebody could get hurt with these. I don't mean to be a drag, but this is against camp regulations . . ." Danni felt her face flushing. She crossed her arms, feeling foolish, but pressed on.

"C'mon now, darlin,'" Clint wheedled, looping his arm around Danni's shoulder. "There's no harm done. We don't need to bring Ahrens into this, now do we? We'll use a cap gun next time. Right, Russell?" he called to his fellow wrangler who reappeared from the shadows. Russell nodded idiotically, baring his teeth in what he must have assumed was a reassuring grin.

Danni moved herself from beneath Clint's arm. "I am not your 'darlin,'" she said shortly. "And I'm serious about this, Clint. This really isn't safe. In fact, it's downright stupid."

Clint's face took on a look of irritation. "Well, let's not make a big deal out of it. It's not like I'm shooting it at the kids or anything. I know the camp regulations as well as you. I'm not doin' anything wrong."

There was little point in arguing further. Clint counted on his charm to work against Danni telling any of the directors that he was fooling with a real gun around the campers. Danni, though not really swayed by Clint's smile, was nonetheless worried about his popularity with the other staff members. If she mentioned anything to anyone, Clint could very well get into some serious trouble. Already feeling a little unsure of how people saw her—did everyone think she was self-righteous?—Danni struggled with what to do. She turned away from Clint silently.

Walking back to the base camp, Danni had time to think over her options. She decided against reporting the matter to anyone. She didn't want to look like a nark, even though she knew that guns were totally against camp regulations. She felt that this once, she could claim ignorance of the whole thing—especially since it was never going to happen again, as Clint had said. That decision made, she blocked out the other thoughts in her head and quickened her pace, determined to put as much distance between herself and Cowboy Camp as possible. She was surprised to hear a call behind her. She turned to see Kevin jogging up the trail. She paused to let him catch up.

"I guess you saw that gun Clint's been waving

around," Kevin spoke without preamble. Danni felt her heart lurch. So much for claiming ignorance.

"Yeah," she responded vaguely, "I guess I did."

"He'd better be careful," Kevin said bluntly. "The kids are getting way too interested in that thing. It's Pace's day off—that's the only reason he has it out."

"Oh," Danni said, silently willing Kevin to keep talking.

"They're taking bets on whether or not you're going to tell," he continued, with a sidelong look at her face. Danni felt her stomach plummet like a frozen boulder.

"Any advice?" she croaked, hating the waver in her voice.

"You need any?" Kevin looked at her incredulously.

"What would you do?" she kept her eyes on the graveled trail.

Kevin sighed and cracked his knuckles. "Somebody's going to get hurt," he said finally. "Clint doesn't show much sense, letting the kids see that thing. It's OK as a prop, but still—" he shrugged.

Danni lifted her shoulder slightly, defensively. "Well, I'm just going to let it go. He said they wouldn't do it anymore. If he does it again, then I'll say something, I guess."

Kevin shrugged. "I don't know, Danni. I hope Clint just locks that thing up."

Danni's day off came and went. Well rested, she approached the end of the week. The Waves Camp staff came in from the lake, looking sunbrowned and tired. They were going to inner tube down the Braxley River, which fed into the long, cool Toscanna Bay. Roseanne barely got a quick wave and hug in to Danni before her duties called her elsewhere.

"Let's make some time to chat on Sunday," Danni called to her as she took off.

But there was no time to chat. On Saturday night Roseanne spent much of her time trying to separate fact from fiction in the wake of a scuffle between one of the Waves campers and a dark-haired boy from Cowboy Camp. According to one account, the Waves camper had started the whole thing. Others argued that the Cowboy camper had been strutting around and had tripped the Waves camper. All accounts agreed that the Cowboy camper had threatened the Waves camper, and had promised to "fix him" before going home. The Waves camper, older and brazen, sneered.

Sunday morning, the usual babble of address exchanges and camper farewells was punctuated by a loud scream. Heads turned and more screams were heard. Danni, in the main lodge building, looked up and thought that someone else had started a water fight. She raised her eyes to the ceiling and sighed. But Eva, outside in the parking lot, had seen a dark-haired boy pull a small gun from a jacket pocket and, with shaking arm, aim it toward a group of Waves campers.

"It was as if he didn't understand what he was about to do." Eva worried the cuticle of her thumb with her index finger. "He just thought he'd get even, never mind that he had a better chance of hitting someone else. He was still mad when Clint took the gun from him! I don't know how he could have known where the wranglers kept the gun." She shook her head. Danni, sitting, hid her shaking knees and swallowed dryly.

"Ahrens will have a few hard words with all of the counseling staff about keeping track of the campers, and making sure to stop incidents before they start. It's definitely a different group, with a lot of the older kids staying for Waves and in the Cowboy program. Doug Pace is meeting with the Cowboy staff this morning, and I'll bet that we'll all hear more about this. Well," Eva sighed, "let me not keep rambling on." She pushed off from the wall she was leaning against. "Staff meeting will be very late this morning."

"Someone could have died," Danni said, and cleared her throat.

"There, but for the grace of God," Eva replied, walking into the staff assembly room.

Danni followed woodenly.

July 20 . . . Sunday

I think I'm going to tear the first page of this out. Perry's attitude problem is the least of my worries. I don't know how else to start . . . I guess this journal is to You, God.

Is there ever a such thing as doing the right thing for the wrong reasons? Was I right in letting Clint just do his own thing? After all, he said he knew the rules just like me . . . but it's never about just one person, is it? Other people knew what he was doing—I mean, Kevin knew, maybe even some of the counselors. I guess that they didn't say anything for the same reason I didn't.

It wouldn't be so bad if this had affected just me, but my wanting to look good in the eyes of other people could have cost a kid his life! Not to mention that would have been the end of my job here, because this place would have been shut down. I feel so stupid! I am so mad at myself, too, because this is just like what Perry said. I totally let Clint walk, even though I knew that he could get into trouble, or somebody else could. But I can't keep saying "I should have," can I? I guess the first thing I need to do is apologize to Perry for being kind of a jerk . . . even though I think he wasn't too cool either. Maybe a true friend tells you the truth, whether you want to hear it or not.

CHAPTER 8

Miserable Christmas

Danni found time on Sunday afternoon to snag the vacuum cleaner out of the hall closet and give her room a quick run-through. Winona's nocturnal wanderings brought twigs, hay, and dust into the room, and Danni felt that the least she could do, since she was never around to clean anything else, was to take advantage of the lull in her activities.

Nosing the machine under the Nona's bed, Danni discovered something soft in front of the roaring machine. Thinking that it was a pair of shoes or a piece of clothing, she reached underneath to retrieve it. She pulled out a brightly wrapped package, then guiltily shoved it back under.

Oh, no! How could she have forgotten! This week was Christmas in July week! This could be a perfect time to further smooth the waters between her and Winona. Hurriedly, Danni switched off the loud appliance and raced out into the hallway with it. Darren Irwin, emerging from his room, held out his hand to borrow the vacuum.

"Thanks. What's your hurry?" he asked Danni as she whizzed back toward her room.

"I forgot that it's Christmas in July this week, and I

haven't gotten Nona anything," Danni responded, pushing open her door.

"Are you seriously getting everybody gifts?" Darren's brows arced incredulously.

"No." Danni shook her head impatiently. "But she's my roomie! Come on!"

Darren laughed. "Well, I guess I'd better get something for Perry then, since he's the closest thing I have to an actual roommate. Maybe I'll wrap up a roll of TP for him."

Danni rolled her eyes and darted into her room.

Christmas in July week was festive. The cafeteria was decked with colorful garlands wound around the posts of the porch and tiny white lights strung around the serving deck. The cafeteria staff dug out red and green napkins from the storage room, and the salt shakers became little white snow people. The campers responded to the festive feel by breaking into impromptu Christmas carols and singing "The Twelve Days of Christmas" whenever possible, and making up a Lupine Meadows version. Danni, who normally loved the holidays, found that she was being driven a little mad.

The worst thing about that particular week, however, was not the excessive red and green decor, or even the fact that Danni and Eva were quickly reworking the program for the week to include a special celebration of Christmas on July 25. The worst thing about that week was the weather.

"No one will believe that it's only 9:30 in the morning," groaned a perspiring Glenda as she wandered listlessly up the hill toward the nature center. "It's got to be at least 90 degrees already."

"No kidding," agreed Danni, blowing out and up toward her bangs in an effort to cool her dripping face.

"Wouldn't you know that it would get warmer instead of cooler for Christmas? Well, at least we'll be air-conditioned up here." Danni wrenched open the heavy glass door of the building.

The girls flopped dramatically against the huge granite stone that stood just beyond the entrance. The stone, once used by the Native Americans for grinding acorns and corn into flour, was pitted with holes and cool to the touch. Danni lay back against it and gave silent greetings to the huge, black bear that loomed over her. Whoever had stuffed the bear had been a top-notch taxidermist, Danni decided. Even with its felt tongue and glass eyes, the beast still looked menacing.

"Well, I guess we'd better get started," Glenda sighed finally, sitting up and dragging the heel of her hand across her forehead. "It shouldn't take too long to haul the animals back to the cafeteria and set everything up."

Danni and Glenda set to work reluctantly. Setting up a winter scene in the dining room with some small stuffed animals surrounding the Christ child's manger had seemed a great idea when the weather was a balmy 80 degrees. Having to haul fur pelts and props down the hill and across the meadow today seemed to be an impossible task. Danni enjoyed working in the cool building, however, and was sorry to find that they were finished in a few minutes.

"Oh, why didn't we bring a truck up here for this?" Glenda moaned.

"Cheer up, Glen," Danni encouraged her. "Think of the legs you'll have when the summer is over."

The air seemed hazy as the girls stepped from the dim interior of the center. From across the meadow the sounds of guitars and singing at Camp Council echoed. Glenda squinted toward the sound.

"Do you think Eva's got a fire going this morning?" she questioned Danni.

Danni gave Glenda an odd look. "No, we never have a fire in the morning. And in this heat? Why?"

Glenda squinted again, and this time she twitched her nose. "Don't know," she replied, a little distractedly. "Smells like smoke somewhere. Let me go up the tower and see what I can see." She put down her boxes. "Back in a minute."

Danni decided not to be left behind. She scooted their boxes into the dubious shade of the nearest clump of weeds and jogged after Glenda. In the morning sun, it was not as pleasant to climb the telescope tower as it was on the numerous velvety-black nights Danni had come up to see the stars. She was perspiring again as she reached the top. Glenda was using a pair of high-powered binoculars to scan the horizon. She turned north, then west, then east. The trees all looked the same to Danni, but she peered out with her arm shading her eyes.

"See anything?"

"Nope." Glenda removed the field glasses. Her mouth had worried brackets along side of it. "I have a bad feeling about this haze, though. I'll have Bill look at it on his way up." She turned to descend the steep ladder.

On the way down the hill they met Bill, who was going up. The heat hardly seemed to affect the tall, fair-haired boy. He frowned and pulled off his "serious scientist glasses" (as Danni referred to them) when Glenda said the word fire.

"I thought it was a little hazy too," he agreed, polishing his glasses absently on the tail of his shirt. "That's just what we *don't* need, with this heat wave starting up. I'll go up and have a look-see." He gave Danni's ponytail a quick tug and hurried up toward the tower.

By lunchtime the bad news was out. Though not on the camp's 960-acre property, there was indeed a brush fire raging about eight miles from the property line. It had started, Mr. Ahrens informed them at lunch, with a tramp logger who fell asleep at his campsite without having fully banked his fire. He had been seriously shaken when he had stumbled into the forestry station, but by the time they got back to his site the fire was out of control.

The executive staff met for an emergency meeting directly after lunch. Eva explained that they needed to have a plan of action in case the fire spread to their own acreage.

"We'll have to evacuate the children," Eva shook her head grimly. "The general staff is gassing up all of the buses, and in the kitchen they're preparing emergency rations. I hope we don't have to use any of these measures."

"Where would we go?" Danni was bewildered, and not a little nervous.

"I don't know—" Eva shrugged. "That's what I'm going to the meeting to find out."

The general consensus was that the campers would be evacuated to the lake, initially. The Waves Camp had adequate kitchen facilities, and if the Base Camp kitchen provided extra food, they would have enough for one meal together. Then the inevitable would happen—parents would be contacted and the staff would bus the children to their home towns.

"That would be awful," Danni complained. "Their whole week would be ruined!"

"Not to mention the fun the office would have wading through all the reimbursement paperwork," Eva agreed glumly. "We all just need to pray that it doesn't happen, and carry on."

Danni sent up an agonized prayer right then and

there. She was terrified of the fire, terrified of the destruction it could wreak. She feared that the beautiful meadow, with its black-eyed Susans, wild daisies, brilliant orange poppies, and fragrant lupines, the gleaming pond with its cool green depths, and all of the dim woods filled with breathless evergreen scent in the afternoon heat would be nothing but a smoking, black, charred ruin.

The mercury in the thermometer outside of the nature center climbed past 95 the following day, and paused at 100 the day after. Camp schedules changed as Gloria reminded the staff of another concern.

"It is not safe to let the kids run around so much in this heat," she said crisply, her own bronzed face glowing in the early morning light.

Through the window of the staff room Danni could see the merciless sun beaming over the meadow. Already it promised to be an unforgivingly arid day. Danni called her attention back to Gloria's words.

"We'll have to open the pool all day, being careful to make the kids get out and reapply sunscreen, especially during the peak sunburn hours between 10:00 and 2:00." Lori Ann nodded as if she had been expecting this. Gloria continued. "We'll need to get some other activities together then, maybe pull out some rainy-day board games that the kids could play in the dining room, show a nature video up at the nature center—"

"Preferably something with snow in it, like that sled dog movie," interjected Bill, and everybody laughed.

Gloria grinned and continued. "And of course, if Bev has any extra activities at the A&C, that would be great, since it is always so cool up there." The arts and crafts director nodded her head graciously.

"The horses are out," Jim Hodges called, making it

more of a statement than a question. Doug Pace nodded, and Mr. Ahrens turned to catch Doug's eye.

"Will you guys be OK down at Cowboy?"

Doug nodded again. "I'll bring them up to the pool once a day, same as always. They'll be OK, with the creek down there. It's always cooler at our end of the meadow anyway. We'll do some roping practice and tell stories in the barn, and have a water fight or something."

Jay Dunstan and Steve Chase decided that their campers would be fine staying up on the hill in their own settlements.

"The archery range is shady anyway," Jay shrugged. "We'll come down and swim on our usual schedule, so I think we'll be fine." Steve agreed as well.

Jim and Kevin, released from their horsemanship responsibilities, gave each other high fives.

"We'll find something for the two of you to do, never fear," Eva leaned forward and grinned at Jim and Kevin. They groaned simultaneously.

"One last thing," Gloria's treble voice rose above the clamor. The staff quieted respectfully. "The last thing is that we have to get these kids to drink water all day—we'll have pitchers of ice water and cups in the dining room with the kids' names on them, so there's not so much waste. It's my goal this week to not have one kid come in with a fever because of dehydration. Heat exhaustion is no fun for big people, either, so don't you guys forget to drink a lot too. That's all from me." Gloria sat gracefully.

The staff kept busy that week as the temperature climbed. On Thursday it peaked at 105. Danni was afflicted with a heat rash that covered her stomach and arms. Her day off found her sleeping restlessly in her darkened room, not even willing to go down to the pool in the choking, smoky heat. She took numerous showers, and called her parents to wallow in her misery.

"Eva picked a great weekend to go to her family reunion," she moaned to Bart. "There's less work to do, but I have less energy to do it!"

The brush fire burned to within two miles of the property line. The firefighters struggled to contain it, but with the excessively dry grasses and low branched trees, it seemed impossible. Ahrens had placed the staff on standby for an evacuation. Every evening, prayer was held in the staff room as the staff gathered to ask for God's intervention on their behalf.

Toward nightfall Danni emerged from her room. Lori Ann and Victor had promised to open the pool for staff members only after campfire. Danni decided to make a quick PB&J for supper, then start out for the pool.

Gooey sandwich in hand, she stopped by the headquarters building to check her mailbox. She riffled through the schedules and announcements from the office, smiled at a good-bye note from Eva, and felt her heart squeeze just a bit when she saw Kevin's precise scribble reminding her that he would be down at the pool after campfire and that she should come by too. Danni blushed, even though no one was there to see it. She decided to go, and promised herself that she would spend more time with Kevin.

Energized, Danni started for the door. Lena opened it from the other side, eyes rimmed red from weeping. Danni stepped back immediately.

"Lena?" Her voice had a strangled quality. Spartan Lena never cried.

"I'm glad I found you," Lena smiled briefly, her grieving face illuminated for a moment. "I was just getting ready to go look in your office. Perry—" Lena reached out a cold hand and clasped Danni's wrist—" Perry was in a car accident today."

Danni was grateful for the cold pressure of Lena's strong fingers. Her stomach flopped, and the peanut butter felt like clay in her mouth. "What happened?" she cried.

"The goof ran into a parked car," Lena chuckled, tears seeping from her eyes.

"A *parked car?*" Danni exclaimed, an insane giggle just under the surface. "Is he all right?"

"He's got a big bump on his head, but he's OK ," Lena responded, wiping tears.

Danni rolled her eyes at the thought of Perry hitting a parked car, of all things. She looked at Lena lovingly. Dear old Lena, whom everybody thought was like a rock, falling to pieces over a little fender bender. She flung a friendly arm about the tall brunette's shoulders.

"Oh, Lena, Perry's gonna be OK! Don't cry. When we get our licenses I'm sure we'll get into little scrapes like this every once in a while too. Come on, come with me down to the pool."

Lena hugged Danni back. "I know you think I'm being silly," she sniffled. "It just could be worse next time, you know?"

Danni blinked in confusion. *Next time?* "There won't be a next time," she reassured her friend.

Lena blew her nose on a wrinkled Kleenex. "You're right. Maybe Victor could drive him. I guess I shouldn't borrow trouble." She smiled waveringly and turned toward the door.

Danni was confused. "Drive him? Where was he going?" she ventured to ask.

Lena faced her with a confused look. "To get his treatments. He'd better have someone drive him there next time. It's just as stupid to die of a car wreck as of leukemia."

For a moment it seemed that the earth cartwheeled. Lena's horrified face swam before her.

"Oh, I'm sorry, I'm sorry," Lena gasped as Danni collapsed, nerveless, against the headquarters door. "I thought you knew. You guys are such close friends, I just thought—" Lena covered her mouth with her hand.

Danni felt the sandwich coming up and sprinted through the door. Now everything was explained—Perry's "cold," his frequent exhaustion, aches, and his pale face. Perry had leukemia.

"Why didn't he ever tell me?" Danni wailed silently.

The rest of the week seemed pointless. Surprisingly, the temperature peaked at a cool and breezy 77 degrees on Friday, the 25th. The fire was contained a quarter mile from the camp property line. Perry's car, totaled, was towed home, and he became the absent butt of the kitchen staff's jokes for hitting a car that wasn't even moving. Danni, hearing all of this, felt herself slip into a suspended world. She could feel nothing. She supposed that she was relieved that the meadow was saved.

A cool, windy Friday evening made the Christmas in July pageant seem more believable than if it had still been sweltering. Gifts were exchanged, and staff members who didn't have after-campfire responsibilities walked through the cabin area singing carols softly, faces lit by tiny votive candles in bowls of sand.

Lena, who had no cabin to subcounsel for, dragged her sleeping bag up from the general staff quarters and parked it in Nona and Danni's room, between their beds. When Danni arrived after campfire each evening throughout the weekend, Lena would be waiting, sitting lotus-style in her flannel nightshirt, silent.

Danni went through her nightly ritual, which grew shorter as her capacity to care whether her teeth were brushed or her face washed diminished. She said a toneless goodnight to Nona and Lena, crashed onto her bed, and fell into a seamless nightmare.

She never cried.

CHAPTER 9

Finding Our Way

No one could believe that it was the last week of the month. The summer, which at one point had seemed endless, was now past the middle. Mr. Ahrens took time to address staff fatigue, and urged the staff to keep their prayer life vigilant. Danni stared at the toe of her shoe and waited for him to finish.

She had not been left alone. At night she was stalked by nightmares—something huge and deadly, menacing, chased her through endless dreamscapes. During the day she was shadowed by friends. In this meeting she sat flanked by Lena on one side and Darla on the other. Roseanne and Kevin sat at the end of her row. Even Victor and Lyly, whose friendship had become a special part of the summer, sat nearby. Gloria, her eyes liquid with misery, sat as far away from Danni as she could. Danni's "Why didn't you tell me?" was still stabbing her in her gut.

"I couldn't!" was all she could say, throwing up her hands in confusion. "I thought you knew, and then Eva told me you didn't. You do understand, don't you, that it wasn't my story to tell?" she looked entreatingly at Danni's expressionless face. "Perry is my patient, after all."

"I know." Danni turned away, offering scant forgiveness. Everyone had known, all summer, but her.

"He actually was fine a few years ago." Lena, who had known Perry longer than any of them, had attempted to defend her friend. "He's out of remission, and I don't think he's ready to admit that he's sick again. Maybe it felt good to have someone treat him . . . normally, you know. Maybe he thought you would have a hard time with it."

Remembering this, Danni closed her eyes for a long moment.

You thought I'd have a hard time with it? Don't you think this is harder, Perry?

The PowerPack meeting was quiet. Marge talked about "letting go and letting God," and Danni squirmed away from the tired cliché. If she had been paying attention, she would have heard Marge discussing that it *was* a cliché, and then the group dissecting what it meant to them. As it was, when Marge gently called her name, Danni no longer had any idea of what the discussion was about. She came to herself, realizing that the group was holding hands for prayer.

"Would you pray for us, Danni?" Marge repeated the question.

For a long moment, Danni deliberated. "I don't think I can," she finally said. She sat with her eyes open, listening to the praises and prayer requests of the group, never knowing that Marge was earnestly petitioning God to touch her heart.

Danni could almost feel the moment that Perry arrived back at the campground Sunday afternoon. Roseanne came into the program room where Danni was attempting to drown herself in work. She stood quietly and waited for Danni to acknowledge her.

"Well, I guess you're here to tell me too." Danni didn't look up, knowing that Rosey's gentle face would show her hurt over Danni's waspish tone.

"Actually, I didn't come to tell you anything." Roseanne stepped over a crate of props and found a place to sit.

Dannielle rubbed her face wearily and sighed. "I'm sorry, Roseanne. It's just that Lena and Darla just left. Anyway, let's start again. What's up?"

Roseanne shifted in her seat. "I just came to see if you're all set up for Inner City week. There will be a lot of older kids here this week. Hm?"

"Yeah," Danni reached out to close a cupboard door. "They're really an edgy group, too. All this wilderness out here and no boundary lines. It makes some of them nervous. Remember last year when it rained for the first three days?"

"Doesn't look like there's any chance of that, does it?" Rosy continued to make casual conversation. Danni found herself biting back her first smile of the week.

"Have you been sent here to stay with me until Eva gets in this afternoon?" she looked up with a wan smile for her friend. "Aren't you wasting time you could be using to stare at the wonderful Tommy? Or the equally wonderful but under-appreciated Alfred?"

Rosy had the grace to blush. "Danni, why do you make it so hard for people to be nice to you these days?" she protested. "I just wanted to make sure that you're OK!"

Danni sat back on her heels and shrugged. "You know I appreciate it, Roseanne. Really. I just don't know what everyone expects. I know Perry's back today, but what am I supposed to do, go running up to him and say, 'Hey, you're sick, and now I know too'? What's that going to get me?"

Roseanne rolled her eyes, envisioning the scene. "Did you ever stop to think why he didn't tell you, smarty?"

Now it was Danni's turn to be sarcastic. "He made it abundantly clear that he thinks I'm too immature for words, Ro," she shot back. "He's all but accused me of being self-righteous and manipulative. I don't guess that I'd be at the top of his list to be informed."

Roseanne stood up, her fair face flushed. "This isn't a popularity contest," she pointed out, shaking her head. "Get real, Danni. I mean, *think* about it. Who would use a potentially fatal illness to choose friends? Perry just didn't want Kevin to know and didn't bother to mention it. I'm *supposed* to be someone special to him. Kat Armstrong, of all of the super-mature, super-sensitive people in the world, even *she* knew! But no, no, don't tell the baby, Danni, she'll end up going home to her—"

"Would you quit feeling sorry for yourself?" Roseanne's voice shot out like a whip. "I can't believe that you'd be this self-centered. *He's* the one who's got leukemia!"

Danni flinched, finally hearing the words. She sat hunched over, hands grasping her elbows. She somehow feared that if she didn't hold herself together, inside she would fly apart.

"I know," she said quietly. She spoke quickly, putting the words out in a rush before her courage died.

"Betti's my stepmom, you know," she began. "My own mother died," she swallowed, "when I was 7. Of cancer. Daddy tried to do his best to not let us worry, but my mom was in so much pain . . ." Danni struggled for control. "I haven't thought about this in such a long time. I just can't stand the thought that Perry . . . I've been such a pill! All we've done is argue." Danni stopped and took a deep breath. Roseanne pulled her up, and led her to a chair.

Danni heard a drawer open, and Roseanne returned to her, pressing thick tissues into her hand.

Roseanne said quietly. "I want to tell you something."

Danni quickly blotted her eyes. She sat, head down,

pleating the remaining tissues with shaking fingers. Roseanne sat across from her.

"I'll bet that you don't know how much Perry really likes you," she began. "Lena has said several times that she wishes that she could be you. Perry loves to tease you. He cares about what you think. He is so impressed with who you are."

Danni shrugged without raising her head.

Roseanne laughed dryly. "Of course, you're the last one to know this," she shrugged. "Anyway, he really likes you. He had other friends that he really liked . . . friends he lost the first time around when they found out he had a potentially fatal illness. Some people can't take the heat, you know?"

"I guess," Danni mumbled.

"I don't think we can ever understand how this—not being sure that you're going to make it—really cuts up your dreams. I would be so angry. There would be so many things I would want to do . . . I mean, Perry totally had plans to see if you were serious about Kevin—that's what he told Lena."

Danni raised a horrified face. "What? Oh, no!"

Rosy plowed on. "Do you see why he couldn't tell you? Who knows, maybe you would have dated him out of sympathy or because you were scared. Or maybe you would've just bailed altogether. He just wanted to take his chances with you seeing just him, not the disease. I guess he just didn't want things to change . . . yet."

Danni shuddered and wrapped her arms around herself. "It's hard not to see the disease." Her voice dropped softly into the stillness in the room. "I don't think there was ever any chance that I wouldn't see it—none of us are blind." She shook her head aggressively to clear her thoughts. "I really wish he had just told me. Now I feel like time's running out. There are three weeks left of the summer, and all we've done is argue and avoid each other. And"—her dry throat absorbed the words—"and I keep thinking, 'Why? At 17, why?'"

Roseanne reached out and caught Danni's hand.

"I want to tell you what I believe," she said softly. Danni was caught by the intensity in Roseanne's voice.

"I know you know all of the clichés, all of the things people say in the face of tragedy. I know that it's impossible to see why God allowed this to happen to Perry. But Danni, when you think of yourself standing beneath the robe of God, you know that everything that he allows to touch you has been . . . well, like approved. Filtered. It may not seem like it now, but God never gives us more than we can bear—and that means Perry too. We can't even imagine how this could bring good to someone, and I can't imagine trying to find that good. I don't think God asks us to like it. On our own power we can't do anything but hate."

"Then, what can we do?" Danni asked bitterly. "Just live, knowing that nothing makes sense?"

"We can do things only through God's strength in us," Roseanne reminded her. "Philippians 4:13. You have to ask God to give you a trust in His plan. There isn't any other way you can ever understand."

Danni digested this is silence. "I just wish . . ."

Roseanne studied her friend. "What would you do differently during the whole summer that you can't do in three weeks?" she asked.

Danni half shrugged again, then smiled weakly. "Is this the 'make the most of the time you have' lecture?"

"Yes, it is," Roseanne replied promptly. "Save me my breath, and just think about it, OK?"

Danni sighed and closed her eyes briefly. "Sure. Thanks, Roseanne."

Roseanne turned to go, then paused at the door for a

moment, her face shadowed by concern. "Sure, Danni. I want you to know that you're in my prayers. If you ever need to talk, or anything . . ." she let the sentence trail off. Danni stood and gave her a tight hug. Roseanne left the room.

By the time Eva returned from her reunion Danni had the campfire props packed and was going up to the headquarters building to see if there was any new mail from the weekend. Eva and Gloria were leaning against the split-rail fence in front of headquarters, watching a pickup game of basketball between two of the boys' cabins. Gloria's expression was guarded as she greeted Danni, and the latter realized that she had been horrible to her friend. Gloria, however, seemed happy to forget the incident in the worship room, and brushed aside Danni's quiet apology. She put an arm around her and let her closeness be a comfort.

Danni's final surprise of the day came just before campfire. A firm knock on her door caused her to scurry from the bathroom, hairspray in hand. She cautiously opened the door and let out a squeal.

"David! You did come! I thought you couldn't make it!" Danni bounded through the doorway to give her friend from the previous summer a huge hug.

"You look great!" David enthused, returning the hug. "Having a good summer?"

Danni smiled briefly and changed the subject. "Where are you staying?"

"I'm bunking up with Darren and Perry for this week, then we'll see if they're ready to kick me out. I'm going to help Bev out with crafts, and hang out with you and Eva. Sound like a plan?"

Danni could only beam. She was ecstatic, and supposed that Eva had to be more than happy.

"Where's Eva hiding herself?"

"She's getting ready to go down to campfire. She just wanted us to have a minute to say hello by ourselves. She told me," and his dark eyes held hers solemnly, "that you've had a rough last couple of days. Is there anything I can do?"

Danni dropped her eyes. She stepped back into her room. David came and lounged in the doorway. Danni set down her hairspray and began fiddling with her ponytail.

"I guess you know about Perry," she began in a low voice.

David's face took on a look of compassion that Danni had to turn away from. She fought the watering of her eyes, took a breath, counted to 10. She continued.

"I just—I'm so messed up by all of this. He never even told me he was sick. He's been acting like nothing's wrong, you know? Like he's going to be OK."

"And you think he won't?"

"Come on, David. People die of cancer every day. My mom died of cancer. I don't believe that you can just ignore the whole thing. Perry's been acting like everything is the same, and it isn't."

David's voice was quiet. "What do you want him to act like?"

"I don't know! I don't want him to do anything, but I want—I don't know . . ." Danni trailed off uncertainly. "I just wish that he had told me."

"You should tell him that."

Danni shrugged. David said again. "Tell him. The sooner you do it, the better you'll both feel."

Danni felt a tinge of guilt. "Both?"

David stepped into the room and gave Danni a big hug. "Yes, both. You both look like you've lost a friend." He stepped back into the hallway and turned to go.

Down the hall a door closed, and Danni smelled Eva's perfume wafting down the corridor.

"Everybody ready?" Eva's smile was tentative as she looked at Danni. Danni flashed her a reassuring smile.

"I'm fine, and I'm coming," she replied to her friend's unspoken question.

Campfire was noisy and rowdy. The campers, not content to stay in their seats, invented new cheers for the campfire games, and did "the wave" to the songs the band played. Danni lost track of the times she saw counselors reach out to retrieve wandering campers. Obviously, bedtime would be a challenge.

"Can I talk you into doing 'bush patrol' tonight, at about 10:00?" Lee Macomber's voice was low and her face harried as she approached Danni.

"Sure," Danni replied uncertainly, giving the girls' director a nervous look. "What do I do?"

"There will be a group of you," Lee assured her, smiling. "You'll just kind of wander out through the cabin area, all the way down to the logging road, and help these rowdy ones to stay where they ought to. They're a wild bunch this week!"

"How long do you want us to do it?" Danni asked, getting into the spirit of things.

"Until about 11:00. Darren and I will be taking the first rounds, until 10:30, with Lori Ann and Victor. They have to get up the earliest to open the pool before worship. At 11:00, Mr. Ahrens will be walking with Marge and a few others. You can start patrolling earlier, if you're free. We could use the help."

The chance to stay up past the strict camp curfew was appealing to many staff members. Eva and David decided to take the first rounds with Lee, to catch up on all the gossip. Danni, after grabbing a dark sweatshirt from her room, hurried to meet up with Lyly, who was a substitute counselor that week. Lena hesitantly joined them.

"I wonder which group Kevin's with," Lyly said. Danni shrugged and looked toward the cabin area.

"Are we supposed to go through the guys' cabin area too, or just the girls'?" Lena wondered.

"I think there are too many lights on still in the guys' section," Danni mock shuddered. "We might see something we don't want to see."

"Hey, are you guys going on patrol? I want to go with you." Kat Armstrong pushed her way into the group, looking from one girl's face to another. Quiet Suzanne materialized beside her.

"I thought you were at the Native Village this week," Lyly looked confused.

"Oh, Running Bear is just going through the usual gig, telling them a story and all. Nobody's going to miss me for an hour or two tonight. The counselors are all up there, and Winona is taking pictures up there." This was said with a sideways glance at Danni.

Danni refused to seem interested. "Hmm," was all she said.

"Well, come on!" Kat shrilled impatiently. "Let's start with the guys' area. Some of them actually are worth looking at, don't you think?"

"Kat! Get real!" Lyly engaged Kat in a teasing argument. The trio started off.

"Um, I want to start with the girls' area. We'll meet you halfway," Lena called out. She linked an arm through Danni's and propelled her toward the upper cabin row. Danni shrugged and went along.

"Now, Danni, I just want to say this," Lena blurted. "Don't be mad. I'm just trying to help."

Danni tried to see Lena's face in the darkness. "What are you talking about?" she demanded with a frown. She squinted up ahead at the trail, and saw a lone figure sitting on a wide stump. In the yellow light of a cabin porch, Danni saw it was Perry.

"He asked me to," Lena whispered, then disappeared into the shadows.

"Wait—Lena!" Danni hissed. Lena ignored her and headed toward the lower cabin rows.

Danni gave a vicious kick to an innocent pinecone. She jammed her hands into her pockets and stalked toward Perry.

"How could you do that to her?" she waved a hand to indicate the retreating Lena.

"Do what?" Perry seemed caught off guard.

"Ask Lena, of all people, to con me into talking to you. She—"

"Wait a minute," Perry broke in. "I asked Lena because I knew she could get you over here. What are you talking about?"

Danni took a deep breath and raised her eyes toward the starry night. She sighed. "Forget it. You're just as dense as you usually are."

Perry grinned. "You're still mad."

Danni shook her head in irritation. "Perry, I am not mad at you." She changed her tone of voice. "How do you feel?" Her eyes took in his thin face.

Perry's smile faded. "I liked you better mad," he said in a low voice. "Don't do that pity thing with me, OK? I'm fine." He jammed his hands in his pockets and tried to control the rush of rage that hit him squarely in the back of his head. He took a deep breath and blew it out. Danni usually was a person he could count on not to speak to him normally; now the false note in her voice jarred him.

Danni's irritation surged back. "I am not pitying you. I just asked how you were. If you don't have anything else to say, I have to do bush patrol." She walked away rapidly.

Perry loped along beside her. "Slow down. I want to talk to you. Don't you have anything you want to say to me?"

Danni spoke without thinking. "*Now* you want pity? I'm sorry you're sick, Perry. Will that do it?"

Perry stopped, stunned. "What is *wrong* with you? Why are you so mad at me?"

"Why didn't you tell me you were sick, Perry?"

"Because it isn't all that important, Danni. Why are you making it seem like I have five minutes to live?"

"Why are you acting like you're never going to die?" Danni heard the words, and clamped her lips together in an effort to recall them.

They stopped for a moment, in the blue-black shadows beneath the tall pine trees. Danni tried to apologize.

"What, you think I'm not acting sick enough? Or serious enough, since you obviously think I'm not going to make it?" Perry's sarcasm stung her. Perry took another deep breath, obviously trying to hold back his rage.

"No! It's not that. I . . . It scares me. My mother . . . passed away. From cancer. Diffuse histiocytic lymphoma. She got a backache one day and then, bang. I didn't know what was really wrong for so long . . . it just seems unfair that you didn't want to give me any warning."

Perry reached out his hand and touched Danni's shoulder. "I didn't know about your mother, Danni. I'm really sorry."

They stood silently for a moment. Perry caught Danni's hand in his, and tugged her back onto the road. They walked in silence for awhile.

"You really think that I'm not going to . . . I'm going to . . . die, don't you?" Perry asked quietly, after some time. "Truth time."

Danni hesitated, cold. "I wish I could say no," she admitted.

Perry blew out a breath. "You have a right to be scared, after what happened to your mother. I know I seemed to be making a joke out of things. Sometimes it scares me, too, and it helps me keep going if I laugh. Everything is way too serious!" He lowered his voice. "I'm sorry I didn't tell you. I'll tell you now, if you want." He stopped, faced her, and took both of her hands in his.

"No," Danni said in a surprisingly sharp voice. She pulled away and continued to walk down the darkened road.

"Well, I just don't want you to obsess on it like Lena does."

They reached the end of the cabin row, and cut through the wooded trail to reach the second row. Lights were more plentiful now, and laughter spilled out of cabin windows. A door opened and two girls in nightshirts ran out onto their porch. Their shrill argument was silenced by a commanding voice from inside, and they returned to their beds. Perry and Danni continued walking, chuckling over someone's wail that they were hungry.

Danni picked up the thread of their conversation. "I think Lena thinks about your . . . illness all the time because you don't. You take a lot of risks you shouldn't. What were you thinking when you tried driving yourself to your transfusion? Gloria would have taken you, or Marge, or anybody! Lena was crying when she told me about your accident. This is really hard for her."

"Who's to say best what risks I should or shouldn't take?" Perry threw his hands up. Danni took back her now sweating hand, and jammed it in her pocket. Perry continued, "I go through this with my mother, with Ahrens, with Gloria! I can't have people pitying me. Lena knows that."

Danni glared at him. His attitude was really irritat-

117

ing her, and she was angry with herself for being angry with him. "What Lena feels is not pity," she said flatly. "You need to think about that for awhile."

Perry gave her a strange look. Danni just raised her eyebrows, and kept walking.

At the end of the second row of cabins they had fallen into a comfortable silence. Nothing had been resolved, but Danni felt more comfortable with Perry than she had been feeling for a while. A kind of relief had rolled through her when the secrets were done away with.

Most of the cabins were dark. Muffled whispers were heard through the trees. Danni looked about sharply. Twigs crunched as Lyly, Suzanne, Kat, and Lena climbed softly up the trail from the boys' cabin area.

"Hi, Perry, where'd you come from?" Kat whispered too loudly. She was shushed, and the group headed toward the headquarters building.

"Did you guys find anyone?" Suzanne looked curiously at Danni and Perry.

"Nope, everything seemed pretty under control in the girls' area. What about you guys?"

"Darren and Lee had already been through," Lyly replied. "What time is it?"

"Almost 11:00." Lena touched the illuminated face of her watch. "I guess I'm going to bed."

Danni gave Perry a hard look. Perry took a step in Lena's direction. He shot Danni an exasperated look, then said with exaggerated politeness, "I'll walk you, Lena."

Lena looked surprised and glanced back at Danni, who appeared to be studying the stars.

"Good night," she called, a little absent-mindedly. She turned away toward the cabin rows.

"Are you going through again? Oh, good, I'll go too." Lyly's enthusiasm had not waned.

"Maybe this time we'll catch somebody," Danni agreed.

The week took on an energetic rhythm. The campers were up at 6:30 to freeze themselves in half-hearted attempts at water aerobics and swimming laps. Then they straggled to line call, where individual cabins tried to outdo each other in raising the flag with style and respect. They charged through breakfast, complained through chores and cabin clean up, then enjoyed Camp Council before rushing off with relief to their morning classes. Having David back at Arts and Crafts revived a little of the joy Danni had felt before learning of Perry's illness. They spent happy times with Eva and Gloria, catching up on news and reminiscing about old times.

Danni stayed busy. Between decorating for events such as the rodeo and doing the daily work for Camp Councils, she and Eva also were laying the groundwork for the end-of-the-summer Celebration. Danni felt honored to be in on the planning. They contacted catering companies and chartered busses to far off places. Danni enjoyed knowing the secrets but was a little disappointed in not having anyone to share them with. Mostly, she hoped that the work she was doing could quiet the continual buzzing in her head about Perry.

Perry sat out on the cafeteria patio in the sunshine. He was watching Lyly's cabin practice for flag lowering, before they went to their cabin for The Quiet Hour. One of the girls brought down a jump rope and was marching and trying to jump at the same time. Her rope slapped up little puffs of dust from the ground. Perry chuckled as he watched Lyly vainly try to explain that double-Dutch jump roping and flag raising would not be a good mix. Flag raising during Inner City Week took on the entertainment properties of a side show at the circus. Perry was glad just to watch.

He rubbed his hands over his arms. He knew he was doing better than he had been for awhile; he wasn't cold nearly so much, but he wore a long-sleeved shirt to cover up the bruises on his arms. He bruised very easily now, and hated to have people see it and drop their eyes or give him pitying looks. Also he was not as tired as he had been. His white blood cell count was trying to stabilize. Still, he was glad that camp was almost over, because having Gloria drive him to town for his monthly transfusion and biweekly checkups was getting to be a drag. His mother insisted that he come home every day off, and he was beginning to wonder why he had fought to come up to camp to begin with. It would all be easier when he was home.

Darren was leading a herd of tough-looking campers outside. Perry nodded to them, unsmiling. He watched Darren talk to them, and was pleased to see their grudging respect for him. Darren accepted no insolence and received very little. Most of the boys were more than happy to speak shyly about themselves, and talk a little bit about their dreams. The tall one, Tonio, stood aloof, seeming to be enraged that anyone would talk to an authority figure.

Perry, observing Summer's cabin and Mike's, decided that counseling was difficult. He only hoped that there would be time for him to try it one day.

Danni sat on her bed, reading mail from home. She felt a guilty twinge as she found her attention wandering from Betti's breezy chat about nothing much, and forced herself to pay more attention to what she was reading. But lately, thoughts of her mother slipped in before she had time to stop them. In her mind's eye she saw her mother, sitting as Danni did now, on the edge of her bed, telling her the news after school. Danni remembered the day her mother had told her that the cat

120

had had kittens, and the animation in her face as she had described each one of them. Danni held on to that memory, trying vainly to stop the others—the hollow-eyed, gaunt woman who had been too tired to climb the stairs, then to sit up in an armchair, then to live.

Danni put down her letter and made a beeline to find someone, anyone, to talk to.

Lena was climbing the stairs as Danni was going down them. "Hi," Danni smiled eagerly. "Were you coming to find me?"

"Um, no," Lena said sheepishly, high color igniting her throat and cheeks.

"Oh," said Danni politely. She wasn't sure Lena would understand anyway. She paused at the balcony on the second floor. Bill was in the staff room, playing a rolling, liquid piece on the piano. Danni hoped that Glenda was with him. She decided not to stop, and passed on to the ground floor.

Danni walked across the sun-bleached patio and squinted out across the meadow at The Tree. A string of horses was tethered there, swishing their tails lazily. Kevin was not to be seen. Danni felt a disappointment so pointed that she actually had a stomach twinge.

She found herself walking to the eastern end of the meadow, toward the pond. As always, the greenish-blue water beckoned. Danni felt rivulets of sweat rolling down her neck. She pushed back her sopping wet bangs, glad for the sunglasses that were almost always perched on her head. The sun held the meadow flat with its depressing heat. Danni wondered if she should turn back. Then she heard a familiar yell, and saw Kevin and his reddish colored mare trotting along from the Lupine House. Danni's face brightened. She beamed at Kevin, her heart in her eyes.

"I was looking for you," she began, as he said, "I've gotta show you what I found." They both laughed and started again. "You first," Danni instructed him after their words had collided again.

"OK," Kevin agreed. "I wanted to show you, I found an owl's nest. I wanted to let Bill know where it was in case the mother doesn't come back. I have only about 20 minutes until I have to get ready for the afternoon riders. Wanna come and see?"

Danni looked at Kevin and was reminded of her mother describing the kittens. His eyes were so full of delight that she felt tears prick hers for a moment. It was like a cloud had passed between the earth and the sun. Kevin mistook her lowered eyes for fear.

"Bo is really gentle, and we'll ride double, even though—" he flicked a glance across the meadow— "we're not really supposed to. I won't let you fall off." He kicked his foot out of the stirrup and held out a gloved hand for her to take. She stepped into the stirrup and hauled herself up on the horse.

"You OK?" He glanced back at her as she settled herself.

"Mostly," Danni responded warily. She felt like she needed a seatbelt.

"You can hold on to me," Kevin said shyly. Danni linked her arms around his waist. She found it difficult to relax and sat as straight as she could as they set off. At first, conversation was limited as Danni tried to keep her seat, worry about crowding Kevin, and talk intelligently. As they entered the woods, however, she relaxed and enjoyed the cool green dimness. Kevin kept the horse to a brisk walk, and they soon found the nest.

"Bill is going to love this," Danni enthused. "Do you think the mother will come back?"

"I guess so," Kevin frowned. "It's unusual for an owl to be out during the day. Maybe I just scared it off, or something."

"Hope so." They stood quietly for a few moments more. Danni wondered if Kev really did know about Perry. She opened her mouth to ask, felt the need to talk about him clogging her throat. Kevin cleared his.

"You know, speaking of Bill, I really haven't seen him a lot this summer—I've had a lot less free time. I wonder if maybe—" here he took off his hat and raked a hand through his disheveled hair—"you wouldn't like to spend some time our last day off this summer with him and Glenda. You know, go to the beach or something?" He studied the trees.

Danni had to change gears. "Oh, yeah, that would be great," she responded lamely. Then, noticing his anxious face, she continued. "And we could ask Roseanne and she could ask . . . someone." Danni caught herself before revealing Rosey's secret. Kevin gave her a relieved look.

"Maybe she'll ask Al."

"Uh, I don't know . . ." Danni stalled.

"Maybe *I'll* ask Al," Kevin smiled innocently.

"Sure, the more the merrier," Danni shrugged, making a mental note to warn Roseanne.

"Now all we have to work out is Bill and Glenda getting the same day off," sighed Kevin.

"I think that for the last day off, it shouldn't be too hard. And if we chose Friday, that clears Roseanne and . . . well, Roseanne can get the day off. If we put in our request now . . ." Kevin turned the horse back toward the camp.

August 11

I can't believe that the summer is almost over. I haven't taken enough pictures, or looked out at the meadow enough. I haven't spent enough time with friends . . .

The Celebration is almost all finished. I guess it'll be great, but I can't get into it. It seems like we shouldn't be partying when Perry's sick. I feel guilty for being healthy. He's tired all the time. He told Eva that he can't come with us. Now I feel really bad.

I can't stop thinking. I wish I could. I keep remembering Mom. Everytime I look at Perry I think of her.

I wish Mom and Dad wouldn't have tried to keep us in the dark for so long. I keep thinking about that ski trip they sent us on. Bart cut his finger on a binding, and I went into hysterics—I still really don't know why. Maybe I knew something was really wrong with Mom, and I couldn't stand one more member of the family being injured. I started having the nightmares that weekend. And then, when we got back she was in the hospital with tubes in her nose . . .

I wish she would have let me know. I wish she would have let us just hang around with her, read to her, just sit with her. She left me long before she died.

I wish she had let me stay.

CHAPTER 10

Love and Learn

The last days of the summer went quickly. Eva and Danni began the interminable task of cataloging, sorting, and boxing props, costumes, and scripts. Danni smiled to herself as she remembered sniffling through the process the summer before. Every costume had brought with it a rush of memories of who had worn it for what play. Each memory had filled Danni's eyes with tears. This summer she was more inclined to breath a sigh of relief as each box was labeled and locked into a cupboard.

The fabulous day off she had planned with Kevin, Bill, Glenda, Alfred, Roseanne, and Tommy was fast approaching. Roseanne suggested that somebody should pick up her mail and bring it out to her, as she, Alfred, and Tommy would be driving from the lake instead of heading back toward camp. Glenda picked up Alfred and Tommy's mail as well. Danni packed the last of her stash of sodas for the three-hour drive from the Lake counties toward the sea. Bill opted to drive his car, since, as he pointed out to Kevin, he wanted to be sure and *get* there. Glenda sat with her feet propped up on the dashboard, cracking pistachios and flinging the hulls out the car window. Kevin fiddled with his guitar for awhile before giving up and plugging into his Walkman. Typically, Danni fell asleep.

Hours later the salt air roused her from her sleep. The overcast sky was a familiar sight. Gulls wheeled in the air, and a sticky breeze lifted Danni's curled hair from the nape of her neck. She sighed happily. She felt that she could live at the beach.

She sat up and rubbed the seat creases out of her cheek. Kevin gave her a lazy smile and closed his eyes.

"So, are we there yet?" she asked.

"'Bout 10 minutes yet," Bill replied in his tour-guide voice. "Did you get a good beauty sleep?"

Danni whacked him on the shoulder in response. He complained about ungrateful passengers abusing drivers. Glenda silenced him with a handful of nuts.

"Yuck. Can't believe you're still eating those," Danni grimaced.

Kevin sat up and groaned. "What I wanna know is, when do I eat?"

Glenda handed back her nearly-depleted bag of pistachios. Kevin munched a moment, then dug around in his backpack for his water bottle. Danni offered him a soda. He wrinkled up his nose at the nuts and gulped down the soda. By now they were pulling into the parking lot. Bill paid the parking fee, and they drove slowly up the road to where the tent campers set up.

"Does anybody see their car?" Bill scanned the cars parked next to the road. A brisk wind blew straight off the sea.

"Tommy drives a blue Ford," Kevin announced. Danni was surprised.

"Do you two know each other?" She twisted around in her seat to ask.

Kevin's expression was noncommittal. "Not really. Just from school."

Danni didn't ask what that cautious look meant. She knew better than to ask Kev too much when he had that non-expression on his face.

When they finally found the campsite, they found Roseanne alone. Tommy and Alfred, it seemed, had gone bodysurfing and would be back in awhile. Glenda and Danni set up the large tent Glenda had brought. They staked it firmly, even though it was behind a bluff and shaded from the wind. Glenda was taking no chances. They found the bathrooms and the coin-operated showers.

"I guess the guys will put up their own tent?" Danni glanced over to where their gear was stacked.

"I think they brought a tarp. Both Kevin and Alfred are into sleeping under the stars," Roseanne replied. "I'm not sure if Tommy will set up his pup tent or not. Kevin can sleep anywhere."

"Well, I'm ready for lunch," Glenda sighed, patting her lean belly. "Let's bring out the cooler and get started."

They assembled sandwiches and dug sodas from their icy hideouts. The gorgeous Tommy graced them with his presence for lunch, then disappeared again into the waves, with Kevin in hot pursuit. Bill hiked up the cliffs to spot sea birds, with Glenda trailing behind him. Danni stripped down to her bathing suit, grabbed her beach towel, and sprawled stomach down on the sand for a nap. After awhile, Roseanne joined her.

"Sure you don't want to come down to the beach and actually get into the water?" she asked Danni plaintively. "I don't wanna go down there by myself."

Danni groaned and opened her eyes. "Roseanne, your brother's down there. It's not like it'll be a private moment."

"That's just the thing . . ." Rosey trailed off.

Danni sat up, grinning evilly. "OK, I see it—I'm the decoy."

"That's not what I meant." Roseanne fidgeted nervously with her beach towel. "Kev doesn't like Tommy, and he's . . . well, I just don't want him to do something to embarrass me. He won't if you're there."

Danni looked at her friend in astonishment. She hardly ever remembered that Kev and Roseanne were twins—it always seemed like Roseanne was Kevin's older sister. Now the tables were turned, and Roseanne was feeling intimidated by Kevin's disapproval. Danni was amazed.

"Roseanne, Kevin wouldn't do anything to hurt your feelings," she exclaimed.

"You don't know him that well yet," Roseanne said darkly. Danni shrugged, disbelieving, and gathered her things.

Alfred visited with them for awhile, then went back to the water. Glenda and Bill joined them at the shore, windblown and perspiring. Bill flopped back on the sand and threw an arm over his face. Glenda peeled off her hiking boots and socks, then scrunched her toes into the warm sand. Alfred and Tommy came out, and Tommy talked Glenda and Bill into coming in. Kevin sat next to Danni and watched Roseanne fidget. Finally, she got up to go in. Alfred followed. Tommy met Rosey with the same friendliness he met everyone else with, and showed her how to bodysurf. Kevin watched for awhile, then turned his attention to Danni. She basked in his company.

The sunset was a spectacular one. The women enjoyed it from the beach, while the men enjoyed it from the campsite where, amid much good-natured groaning, they were preparing supper. After they ate, Bill built a little fire, and Kevin felt obligated to bring out his guitar.

The peaceful end of a week brought a certain quiet to the group. Everyone put on a sweatshirt and huddled in closer to the fire as the light faded.

Roseanne and Kevin started singing one of the praise songs they sang at campfires. Everyone joined in, watching the fire and feeling the closeness of friendship. They continued singing softly, voices blending and harmonizing. Danni got sleepy first, and excused herself to go to bed. Kevin walked with her to the tent and gave her the best goodnight kiss she had received yet. She floated off to sleep. Glenda and Bill walked awhile in the moonlight. Glenda got cold and gave up, giving Bill a quick hug and trotting back toward the warmth of her sleeping bag. Bill watched her go and wondered if he hadn't better go after her someday. Alfred disappeared somewhere with Kevin.

Roseanne and Tommy were the last around the fire. Roseanne felt awkward—how do you relate to your dream guy in the flesh? Tommy talked for awhile, then told her he thought he'd better get his stuff together and go to sleep. He leaned over and gave her a big hug, then got up to go.

Rosey saw that he had dropped his wallet from the pocket of his shorts. She reached over and picked it up, noting the smooth calfskin leather. She knew she should call him back but before she did she thought that it wouldn't hurt to look at the pictures he had inside. She opened his wallet and found family pictures and school shots of people she didn't know. She especially studied the girls.

Roseanne's conscience began to needle her. If Tommy had found her purse she would hope that he wouldn't go through everything in it before giving it back to her. She sighed and started to close it. A metallic gleam caught her eye; she opened his billfold again, frowning. Was that—*a condom?* She peered closer. Two condoms, in foil wrappers, nestled in amongst his money. Roseanne was shocked. Face aflame, she closed the wallet immediately.

"Uh, Tommy?" she croaked. "You dropped your wallet. I'll leave it on this log here, OK?"

"Oh, thanks," Tommy called back from the depths of his small tent.

"I'll get it," Kevin called as he materialized from behind Roseanne. He began to bank the fire.

Roseanne waited in silence as Kevin worked.

"See everything you wanted to?" he asked finally.

Roseanne glared at him for spying on her, then wondered if he knew what she had found.

"I was just looking at his pictures," she defended herself.

Kev shrugged. "He seems like a decent guy," he admitted.

Roseanne sighed. "Yeah, he does, doesn't he?" She stood up and shoved her hands in her pockets. Kevin looked up at her.

"What's up?" he asked quietly.

"Nothing," Roseanne looked away.

Kevin said, "Hmm," and stood as well. Roseanne found she had nothing else to say.

"Goodnight, Kevin." She turned to go. He caught her arm and pulled her into a bone-crushing hug. She blinked back tears suddenly, remembering the "twin power" that they had joked about when they were younger. Kevin knew something had gone wrong.

"Keep an open mind," Kevin cautioned her before letting her go.

Open to what?

"Are you guys turning in already?" Alfred's voice was low. "Wanna sit for awhile, Roseanne?"

130

Roseanne met her brother's eyes. "I was just going to bed," he answered Alfred.

"Rosey?"

Roseanne pretended not to notice the suggestion on his face. "I'm hittin' the hay," she announced. "'Night, Alfred."

In her sleeping bag, Danni was floating through walls of water, somehow not getting wet. She saw Bart and her father, and then she saw someone swimming up ahead of her, in a blue corridor walled with waves. She knew it was her mother.

"Wait," she commanded her mother. "Hurry, hurry, hurry," she chanted to herself. Instead of herself speeding up it seemed that her mother heard her say "hurry" and zoomed ahead.

"I can't go that fast. Mom, I can't keep up. Mama—"

Suddenly the menacing stalker was there, coming between Danni and her mother. She tried to put on brakes and stop herself, dodge IT, crawl beneath IT, still reach her mother. But then IT caught her, slowed her down. IT held her down beneath a wall, and suddenly Danni wasn't just getting wet. She was drowning.

Great, gulping, sobbing breaths came through the tent. Danni sat up to hear who could be making that awful sound. She put her hand on her forehead and felt the perspiration there. Then the nightmare came crashing back down on her. She pulled on a sweatshirt and pushed her feet into a thick pair of socks. She hoped her stretch pants would be warm enough. She had to get out of the tent. It wasn't fair to wake the others. Glenda was having a bad time pretending she didn't care about Bill. Roseanne had been very down when she came in, and wouldn't talk. It wasn't fair to wake the others with her misery. She quietly unzipped the tent and crawled out.

The moon was directly overhead, and the tide was coming in. Danni sat down on a bit of driftwood and took a deep breath. She hoped she hadn't wakened anyone. She looked out at the blue-black water and remembered the fuzzy image of her mother in the dream. She closed her eyes and concentrated fiercely. Her mother was there. Brown hair, usually sprayed back into two huge wings that framed her face. Green-gray eyes and a straight nose. Thin lips, even teeth. There. That was her mother. Danni let out a sigh of relief.

The white roar of the water was soothing. Danni found herself humming a snatch of an old song that she didn't recognize for a moment. The words came to her, and she sang under her breath for a moment. Then she laughed as she listened to herself. She remembered her mother walking around the house, dusting things when she came home from work. She had always hummed. Betti whistled and sang too, but it was different, more tuneful. Her mother had always sung just under her breath, as if she had a continual song going on inside of her. There were so many little things about her mother that had made her who she was. Danni strained to remember them. She had to remember them . . . would anyone else? Would someday Perry's family strain to remember the small, special things about him?

Danni felt the beginnings of tears, the slow, leaky kind that continue long past one's ability to wipe them away. She put her head down and let them come. There was no rightness in the world, no fairness. Perry actually had liked her, and she had no way to know how to react to that kind of like. She could not imagine romance in the face of a terminal disease. Then she thought of Lena, who had been trying to get Perry's attention since last summer. Now he was too angry and complicated to even see her. It just wasn't right. Danni felt for the pocket of her fleece sweatshirt. She fumbled out a wadded tissue and mopped her eyes. The tears fell twice as fast.

Danni was hiccoughing now, digging her fingers into her hair. Sometimes it felt like everyone was walking around in total darkness, and at any moment someone could fall and never be missed. She and Eva had been working feverishly on packing and putting the finishing touches on the Celebration for this year. A larger budget had allowed them to charter buses for a day at Six Flags, with an evening BBQ at a dude ranch the night before. Staff everywhere were gearing up for the big party, begging Danni to drop hints, and spreading wild rumors. Perry had indicated to Eva that he would not be able to join the group. Danni's gaiety had collapsed like a soap bubble. What were people doing celebrating when Perry was facing death? How could she ever laugh?

A smoky blanket dropped across her shoulders. Danni shuddered. She hadn't realized how cold she was. She blew her nose and tried to speak. Two warm arms pulled her close, and warm fingers wiped the tears from her cheeks. No questions were asked. Kevin closed his arms around her and held her.

After a long time he broke the silence. "I'll bet you wonder how I knew you were down here."

She nodded, shrugged, blew her nose again. He paused. "Roseanne got me up."

At her sound of dismay he gave her a squeeze. "I'm glad she did. I don't think I'd feel too great if I woke up tomorrow and found out you'd frozen to death out here." He paused again. "If it helps you any, I thought Perry was wrong. I knew about this since the beginning of the summer, and it's still hard for me. I know how you feel about him, so I asked Perry if he could come with us today—and he told me that sleeping was really uncomfortable in a bed, much less on the ground."

Two more tears seeped out onto Danni's cold cheeks. She swallowed hard as Kevin continued.

"If I had known that you didn't know . . . I would have at least talked to him. But he didn't mean to make it harder on you, Danni. I know that much."

Danni buried her face in her arms again, and Kevin just held her, made soothing small talk about the tide and the moon, talked about his plans to come and see her later in the year.

A thought had been struggling into being in Danni's mind. She straightened up. Kevin let her move a little ways away from him. Her voice was scratchy when she spoke.

"Would it bother you very much if I didn't go to the Celebration this year?"

Kevin bent and peered at her. "Don't you have to?"

She shook her head. "Eva and I have finished the planning, really. As long as David is there to help her out, I don't really have to go."

"You're going to spend some time with Perry, then?" Kevin's voice had not changed. Danni took a careful look at him. His face in the moonlight was serious, his eyes shadowed.

"Would it bother you?'

Kevin shrugged. "It wouldn't be as much fun, but I guess I'd see you when you got home. How would you get home, anyway?"

Danni leaned against him for a moment. "I can always take a bus. It's just something I need to do. I just want to spend some time with Perry before . . . or, I mean, if . . . well, while I have some time."

Kevin looked away uncomfortably. "It's not like there'll be much to do," he informed her. "When people are sick they just sleep and stuff. I think you should go if you want to, but—"

"But don't think I'm going to make a difference. I

know." Danni tried not to be disappointed in Kevin's lack of enthusiasm. He gave her a hard hug and told her she should go back to bed. She sat for a little while longer, thinking, then made her way back over the cold sand to her tent.

It was a little harder than she had thought it would be to break the news to Mr. Ahrens Sunday morning. Eva had taken it well, all things considered, and had pointed out that David would be a huge help with whatever she needed. David had assured them both that he was glad to help, and that any excuse to hang around Eva was welcomed. Mr. Ahrens was not so easily convinced. He insisted on asking Eva several times if she was sure, then spoke privately to Danni about responsibility and following through. Eva finally rescued her, and hauled her down to the office for last-minute reassurances.

"This is really only a few days of fun stuff; it's not that important," she told her assistant. "David will be a real help to me if anything goes wrong. Besides, it may be really important to Perry."

"I hope it will be," Danni sighed.

"What do you mean, hope?" Eva made a face. "Haven't you told him yet?"

"No . . . I wanted to be sure I could do it, first. Now I feel a little nervous—it's like, 'Hi, can I invite myself over to your house and spend a few days with you and your family?' I feel really dumb."

Eva rolled her eyes in exasperation. "You had better go and ask him," she laughed. "I'd hate for all of Ahrens' worry to go for nothing."

Perry was nowhere to be found in the kitchen, or in Darren's room on the third floor. Danni felt a little frantic as she saw all of the bustle of activity going on around her—the dining room had been turned inside out, and a sea of tables and chairs littered the patio. Smells of bleach and wax filled the air. The kitchen was being disinfected, and crews armed with mops and pails were moving through the bathrooms. (Danni gave these people a wide berth.) After having asked the crew cleaning cabins, and called up to the A&C and nature center, Danni began to believe that he was already gone. Then she found Lena vacuuming the staff room and had to shout three times over the roar of the machine to be heard. Lena said that she thought that Perry was in the general staff quarters, packing his things.

The staff quarters were a disaster. Although it was early, many of the work crews were finished, and the showers were pushing out billows of steam. Danni hesitated in the lobby between the men's and ladies' quarters. She knew the staff rule about ladies staying out of the men's quarters. She shifted impatiently, and then seized the first male she saw.

"Charlie! Hi, would you mind seeing if Perry is in there and tell him to come out?"

Charlie looked startled. "Sure. Could you . . . well, since you're right here, could you yell into the girls' quarters and tell Shyanne I'm going to help finish up at the nature center?"

"No problem." Danni opened the heavy wooden door.

When she came back, Perry was standing next to the bank of phones that graced the far wall of the lobby. He smiled tiredly at her, and started in on his usual banter.

"So, you finally decided that you missed my smiling face, huh? Fancy you coming all the way here to see me."

"Perry . . ." Danni rolled her eyes as he continued teasing her.

"What's up?" he finally asked her.

"I—uh, well, I was hoping . . . Well, I heard you aren't going to Celebration."

Perry's expression stilled. "Yeah," he sighed. "I'm just not sure I can handle Six Flags." At her startled look he reassured her, "I haven't told anyone, and Ahrens only told me so that I'd be able to make an informed choice about whether or not I could go. Aren't you guys supposed to be leaving in three hours?"

"Well, yes . . ." Danni stalled.

"Oh, Danni," Perry sighed and crossed the room to stand near her. "Don't tell me you're trying to come here and talk me into it, or say a long good-bye."

"Actually, no." Danni forced a bright note into her voice. "Actually, I came to ask if I could spend some time with you, if you wouldn't mind."

"What do you mean?" Perry seemed cautious as he looked at her.

"I mean, I thought that I'd just spend a few days with you, since we haven't gotten to spend a lot of time this summer—and we live so far from each other. I can take a bus home after a few days. I know you get tired pretty easily, so I won't stay long."

"Danni," Perry grinned, "What would Kevin think? You've got to be kidding."

Danni's face turned scarlet. "No, I thought that this was a good time, since school hasn't started yet, and I know we'll both be busy soon, and . . . well, if you don't want me to come, I'll . . ."

Perry interrupted again. "You mean you want to come today? And skip the Celebration?"

Danni nodded. "If it's something you want to do."

Perry's eyes glowed with elation, but then his guard came up. He shook his head. "It won't be much fun. I mean, I'd love the company, but I'm just going into the hospital on Monday for tests. I have to check in for a day. It really won't be anything but boring. Don't worry about it, Danni. I'll be at the Celebration next year. It's no big deal."

Danni looked away from him for a moment. At one time in her life she would have applauded Perry for being brave, and told herself that she had tried to do the right thing and that since she had tried and he had refused, she was off the hook. She smiled a little to herself. She was not like that now.

"I'd like to come today," she repeated, looking out at the rolling meadow under the brilliant blue sky. "Call your mother."

She refused to look at Perry until he moved toward the phones. Then she watched him as he dialed and spoke. His face showed his excitement. His mother sounded unsure, but eager to please her son. She promised to have a guest room ready. Perry's tired frame straightened. He told Danni to meet him at 4:30 p.m. in front of the lodge. She promised to be ready by then.

It was a different departure for Celebration than Danni had experienced her first summer. Exhausted staff with damp combed hair fresh from the shower piled their dusty belongings into cars and lined up behind Mr. Ahrens' truck. In all of the hustle, very few people noticed that Danni was standing around not taking part. Marge Ahrens caught Danni in a tight hug and told her that she was proud of her. Perry was sitting on the porch of the lodge. Lyly and Victor came by to say good-bye. Danni took advantage of the confusion to make her way through the crowd to Kevin and Roseanne. Kevin put on a smile for her. Lena looked a little crestfallen when she heard Danni's plans, but smiled at her gamely. Danni wished she had the words to reassure her. Darla and Lena were riding with Kevin, as Roseanne had accepted Alfred's offer to ride to the rendezvous point in his battered Volvo. Roseanne's eyes were enormous with unspoken thoughts. She made Danni promise to call the minute she got home. Shyanne and Summer were escorted into Charlie's restored Mustang. Danni swallowed back tears at seeing the chain of taillights make their way down the mountain. Amid clouds of dust and much honking and shouting, the group took off.

The camp was silent. Danni felt like she was underwater. She sat down next to Perry on the bench. Perry sighed and closed his eyes. Danni wondered if she had done the right thing.

Perry reached over and closed his hand around Danni's. They sat quietly for awhile. Then Perry opened his eyes.

"Hey, Danni?" She turned toward him.

"Thanks."

Danni nodded, and felt her tension unwinding. She knew that she had done right after all.